MW00829909

To hell With Hallmark

Brad Ricks

Copyright © 2024 by Brad Ricks

All rights reserved.

No part of this publication may be reproduced, distributed, or transmitted in any form or by any means, including photocopying, recording, or other electronic or mechanical methods, without the prior written permission of the publisher, except as permitted by U.S. copyright law. For permission requests, contact

The story, all names, characters, and incidents portrayed in this production are fictitious. No identification with actual persons (living or deceased), places, buildings, and products is intended or should be inferred.

Book Cover by Christy Aldridge

Illustrations by Crystal Baynam

Editor Terri Ricks, Crystal Baynam

Dedicated to my grandmother Jessie Kruger
She loved her Hallmark Christmas movies

CONTENTS

INTRODUCTION

Welcome to Hallmark, VT.

You may think you've never heard of Hallmark, VT, but that's not true. There's a whole channel that makes Christmas movies based on the happenings of our little town.

Yes...it's that town. The town where it snows every Christmas Eve at exactly the right moment. It's surrounded by luscious trees and picturesque landscapes. The town that young women leave to find success in the big city only to return and rekindle that lost romance on the most magical of nights. The town where the most eligible bachelor is a thirty-year-old widower with a young daughter who also happens to be the town's handyman. The town where the courthouse sits in the center of the town square, and the annual Christmas tree lighting ceremony is attended by everyone. Mistletoes and ribbons hang on every street-lamp.

Oh, and let's not forget the Christmas Cookie competition and the occasional secret prince searching for true love.

Story after story is birthed from our small town. The locals here believe God has truly smiled on their little slice of heaven, allowing us to bring Christmas cheer, joy, and happiness to all who pass through.

Hallmark is truly an amazing place.

That is... until now.

DIMPLES FOR THE HOLIDAYS

Jenny made sure her gray coat was buttoned up before tossing the red scarf around her neck. With her toboggan pulled snuggly over her ears, she grabbed the small stack of books she planned on reading over the next few days. As the librarian for the Hallmark Public Library, she had her pick of whatever she wanted to read.

Lately, her favorite books had been romance. The holidays always seemed to put her in a romance kind of mood. She guessed it was a side effect of turning thirty and still being single. As soon as the snow started to fall and the Chamber of Commerce put up the red ribbons tied in bows on the streetlamps, or the holly and mistletoe along the sidewalk, or the Christmas lights all around the park, she felt that pang of longing in her heart.

She wished there was someone she could spend the holidays with.

With this weekend's three books under her arm, she reached into her purse and pulled out the key to the library's front door. Her slender hip hit the crash bar on the glass door, swinging it open. A brisk breeze hit her face, sending a dusting of snow her direction and into the library's foyer.

Jenny grabbed the thin glass door frame and pushed it closed. She leaned against it, slid the key into the lock, and twisted it closed.

In the glass, she saw her reflection. Her glasses had slipped down her nose as she locked the door. She pushed them back up against her face. Tufts of her long brown hair escaped from the sides of the toboggan, and she tried to shove them back in place before giving up all together.

"Well, Ms. Pearl," Jenny said to her reflection. "Ready for another lonely December weekend?"

"Of course, I am." She answered herself in a deeper voice, pretending like she was actually having a conversation.

She fumbled with her purse, trying to drop the keys back into their appropriate compartment. As she did, one of the books began to slide out from under her arm. Jenny awkwardly shifted her body, trying to stop it from falling. If one went, they all would.

With her feet at a weird angle and her arms attempting to regain the falling stack of books, she almost had it when something large, white, and hairy bounded toward her. It ran straight into her, catching one of her legs and knocking her completely off balance. The books tumbled out from under her arms, and she twisted in a circle.

Her world spun around. She felt herself falling onto the pavement, but then she stopped as if she was suspended in midair.

Her glasses had slipped down her nose again, and the toboggan had worked its way almost to her eyes, obscuring some of her vision.

"Don't worry," a soft-spoken male voice said. "I've got you."

Slowly, she floated back to her feet.

"Cooper. Bad dog," he said. Despite the chastising words toward the dog, his tone was playful.

Back on her feet, Jenny adjusted the toboggan and pushed her glasses back to her face. Her vision cleared, and she saw the newcomers for the first time.

Cooper was large and happy. She recognized his breed as an English Cream Golden Retriever. Cooper, obviously full of energy, bounced back and forth waiting to play. Just seeing the expression on the dog's white face filled her heart.

Cooper's owner, though, made Jenny's heart flutter. He had dirty blond hair that curled out from under a ball cap. He towered over her by at least a foot. A smile beamed from ear to ear, and cute dimples pierced each cheek. He was the perfect man depicted in every sappy romance book she'd ever read. The one who always swept the girl off her feet. And he did just literally catch her as she was being swept off hers.

At the thought of books, she remembered hers on the ground and immediately dropped to get them.

"Here, let me help you with those," he said, and bent down as well.

"No, it's perfectly fine. I've got it," she replied, her hands reaching as fast as they could to gather them.

His hand reached for one of the titles at the same times as hers did, and their fingers gently brushed against each other. Pure energy surged from that slight touch straight through her body. She became starkly aware of how frumpy she currently appeared. Her hair stuck out of the toboggan and she suddenly hated herself for wearing it.

With all three books in hand, she quickly stood back up. As she did, Cooper bounded next to her, catching her back foot. Cooper's owner sprang to action, and for the second time, saved her from falling onto her pride.

"Thank you, Mr...?"

"Stills," he finished as he steadied her on her feet. "Glenn Stills." He held out his hand.

She grabbed it and shook. "Thank you, Mr. Stills. I appreciate your help." Holding his hand, she felt that same electricity again. Her hand lingered, and she embarrassingly pulled it to her side.

"Please, call me Glenn. And that fur ball of energy is Cooper." He pointed to Cooper spinning in circles in the snow. "I'm really sorry he knocked you over. Twice. I only just moved here a few days ago. Thought a nice walk around town would help him get some of his energy out and help me to learn the lay of the land. As soon as we turned the corner, he took off."

Cooper, as if he knew Glenn talked about him, strolled over and stood in between them.

Jenny bent down and rubbed Cooper's fur with her free hand. "Oh, it's okay. He was just excited to be out in the snow." She stood and eyed the books under her other arm. One of the covers had a tear on it.

Glenn followed her eyes. "I'm sorry about your book. I'll give you the money for it."

"Don't worry about it. Actually belongs to the library."

"Well, then I'll get a new one for the library. Do you work here?" he asked, pointing to the small building.

"Yes, I'm the librarian. Jennifer Pearl." She held her hand back out, he grasped it, and gave it a shake. She was sure to pull it back quickly and not let it linger this time. "I need to get going. You two have a nice jaunt around town. Go by the park. Plenty of open space for him to run and snow for him to play in."

"The park," he repeated. "Will do."

Glenn and Cooper strode down the sidewalk away from Jenny.

She also started in the opposite direction, headed for her house.

"It was nice to meet you, Ms. Pearl," he hollered. "Catch you later?"

She turned her head around and smiled, waving. She hoped the darkness hid her blushing cheeks.

"Jenny, you're such an idiot," she chided herself when she stepped into her small townhouse only two blocks from the library.

She grabbed a small remote and clicked a button, sending the lights on the Christmas tree soaring to life. She dropped the books on her coffee table, unbuttoned her coat, and flopped on the couch, lying sideways and splaying her arms out. One reached to the ceiling, and the other touched the floor.

"He was gorgeous and had a cute dog. Why didn't you talk to him more? Why didn't you ask him for his number?"

Jenny glanced at the stack of books on her coffee table and frowned.

"Why couldn't Jane Austen have written my life for me?"

She closed her eyes and pictured his sweet smile with the dimples on each cheek. His soft green eyes. Those slight blond curls spilling out from under his hat.

Jenny sighed and resigned herself to her books for the weekend.

"Guess I'll just read about true love and romance instead of experiencing it."

The next afternoon, Jenny threw on her coat and scarf and stepped outside. She had one book and a bottle of wine down. As she went to the next book and bottle, she realized one of those components was missing.

The brisk, December air sent a chill over her slender frame. Her mother had always told her she wouldn't be so cold if she put some meat on her bones. It didn't matter how much she tried, though, she was blessed (or cursed depending on the viewpoint) to have a fast metabolism. The wind blew straight through her coat, and she wrapped her arms around her body, hugging some warmth into her.

With a glance down the street, she strode to the corner grocer just across from the library. She watched her step along the sidewalk. With the snow falling more and more, the town had begun to lay salt. It kept the ice at bay, but the sidewalks were still wet which added their own layer of slick.

She turned on 2nd, and the library lay straight ahead. Corner Grocer sat on the corner of Main and 2nd. She hopped off the sidewalk and trotted across 2nd. As she opened the door, the usual bell dinged.

"Hey Jenny," Joe said from behind the counter. He was short and stocky. His bald hair with a few strands of gray holding on for dear life could barely be seen over the counter. "How's your Saturday?"

"Same as usual, Joey," she answered and marched her way straight past the Christmas decorations and up to the wine aisle.

"Still burying yourself in books, huh?"

"It's my job. The town librarian has to stay well read," she said. She slid out two bottles of Merlot and sauntered back to the counter.

"Books and booze, I see. When you going to stop reading about stuff and actually experience it?"

She placed the two bottles on the counter. "The wine helps with that. If I'm tipsy while I read, my brain might think I actually did do the stuff. Besides, zip it, Joey. Just ring me up, will you?" She smiled at him.

"One of these days, Jenny, you're going to find some guy, or girl if that's your thing, and forget all about those books. Go travel the world and leave Hallmark behind. You'll be writing the books instead of reading them."

"That's the dream," she said. She paid for the wine and grabbed the paper bags holding her bottles. "Later, Joey. Tell the missus I said hi."

"Will do."

With her two brown bags in hand, she turned her back to the door and pushed it open. The bell dinged again, but then the door abruptly stopped.

"Oof!" someone cried out from the other side.

Jenny quickly spun around, nearly dropping the two brown bags.

Glenn Stills stood on the opposite side of the door with his hands in front of his face, cupping his nose. From his hand, a leash draped down. Cooper stood next to his owner.

"I'm so sorry," Jenny said. She sat her bags on the ground next to the Corner Grocer.

Cooper bounced over to her, furiously wagging his tail.

Jenny stayed crouched and rubbed her hands over his white fur.

"We've got to stop meeting like this," Glenn said, still holding his nose. With it pinched, he sounded like Snuffleupagus.

"How bad's your nose?"

He moved his hands away and wiggled it. "Sore but not damaged. My pride holds that title." He glanced down at Cooper. "I see I've been betrayed by my own dog, and to my violent attacker no less."

She couldn't help but smile. He was definitely charming. She glanced up at his face and saw both dimples on full display, accenting his smile. She reached over, grabbed her two bottles of wine, and stood back up.

"Well, I need to get going," she said and started past Glenn.

"Wait, Ms. Pearl," he said, halting her in her tracks. He started talking, rambling almost, and as he did, his words flew out faster and faster. "I don't know if it was fate or what that had you open the door directly into my face, but I'm glad that it did. I kicked myself last night for not asking if you had dinner plans. Now, I don't know if you have a boyfriend, and if you do, I'm really sorry, but I'd be remiss if I passed up this opportunity to ask you if you'd like to join me for dinner." He paused and took a deep breath.

Jenny couldn't tell if the cold weather caused the redness in his cheeks or the embarrassment for blurting all that out at once. She glanced down at her two bottles of wine and contemplated what her evening was actually about to look like. The next book on the coffee table. The open-sliding-toward-empty wine bottle that would be in front of her. The silence of her living room illuminated primarily by the Christmas tree. For some, that quiet solitude might sound like heaven, but to her, it was a rinse and repeat of every other night, and it sounded lonely. Boring.

"Dinner would be nice," she finally said.

Glenn's face beamed with delight. "That's wonderful. Do you have a favorite place? I'm afraid I don't really know what's good around here yet."

"Well, you obviously know where the library and grocery store are. Around the corner, about another block down Main, is Luigi's. Meet me there at seven?"

"Seven at Luigi's. It's a date. Come on, Cooper. Back to the house, we go. I need to unpack something nice to wear."

And I have to find something nice to wear.

"So, you've lived here all of your life?" Glenn asked. He had just finished the last bite of lasagna and eased back against his chair.

"Born and raised." She twirled her fork around the last of the angel hair pasta on her plate. She had given up trying to finish it a few minutes before, instead opting to simply play with it as they talked.

"This town is like Norman Rockwell met Thomas Kinkade. It's quiet. Everyone I've passed on the street says hi. Main Street with all its decorations for Christmas. I never knew a place like this existed outside of the movies."

"Hallmark is a magical place. God smiles on our little spot on Earth, that's for sure. And you've definitely moved here during the right time. This town really comes alive during the holidays. In a few days, there'll be the Gingerbread Cookie Throwdown. The cookies are simply to die for. And just wait until Christmas Eve. Everyone gathers around the Christmas tree in front of the courthouse. We pass out candles and sing 'Silent Night'. Oh, and this year, at the amphitheater, we have a local band playing. They're a pretty decent rock group during the rest of the year, so I can't wait to hear their version of 'Carol of the Bells'.

"A rock Christmas concert. Doesn't that just sound wonderful?"

She heard the excitement in her voice. This was her favorite time of year. She realized how much she sounded like a fangirl and decided to switch gears.

"Okay, enough from me. What brought you here?" Jenny asked.

She gazed into his eyes, realizing she was getting lost inside of them and not caring.

"Well, I've always moved around a lot. Never been one to stay in one place too long. Lived in upstate New York for a bit, had a brief stay in New Hampshire. Most recently, I was in Rhode Island."

"Rhode Island? Did you hear about that girl that was murdered in Rhode Island? Sad when someone is killed around the holidays."

Glenn's eyes shifted slightly. "I love the decor in this place, by the way. So very quaint and authentic. Have you ever been to Italy?"

"No," she answered. "Maybe one day. I don't really like to travel alone."

He picked up his wine glass, holding it slightly above the table. "To not traveling alone."

Jenny grabbed her wine glass and clinked it against his. "To not traveling alone," she repeated. She downed the last of her wine, watching as he finished off his.

With the bill paid, the two left Luigi's. Jenny grasped Glenn's arm as they strolled. She took in the lights and the light snow. Everything had a haze around it, a new glow. A few townsfolk ventured the streets as well. Jenny recognized their faces and gave them a smile and a nod.

As a beautiful, black-haired woman with soft white skin wearing overalls approached, she said, "Hey, Yvonne. No calls tonight?"

Yvonne smiled, her bright red lipstick accentuating her luscious lips. "All quiet so far. Enjoy your date."

"Oh, I am," she said, as they passed each other.

"Friend of yours?" Glenn asked.

"We've known each other for a while."

"She was dressed odd for a night on the town. Overalls?"

Jenny laughed. "She drives a tow truck. Don't judge a book by its cover, Mr. Stills."

They continued their stroll. As they went under a lattice arch, Glenn came to a stop.

"Something wrong?" she asked.

He eyed her, staring into her soul. "Not at all. Just noticed that there's a mistletoe above us."

She glanced past him to the garland hanging above. Sure enough, a mistletoe dangled from the lattice that stretched over the sidewalk. "Yes, there is."

He leaned forward and gently placed his lips on top of hers. Jenny could've sworn she floated off the ground.

The kiss lasted only a few seconds, but during that brief moment, the world stopped spinning.

As their lips parted, she gazed into his eyes. "I have another bottle of wine at my place. Care for a glass?"

Those dual dimples showed up on his face again. They continued hand in hand with her leading the way.

Once inside Jenny's place, Glenn pulled her close and kissed her again. The two were intertwined within moments, stumbling to get through the entry way and into the living room.

After a few minutes of heated making out, petting, and groping, Jenny pulled away, holding Glenn at arm's length.

Panting, she said, "Wait here a moment. I need to visit the lady's room. My bedroom is just down that hall. Give me a few minutes, then head that way."

Glenn took a moment to still his own racing heart. "As you wish."

Jenny sprinted down the hall, leaving Glenn alone in the living room.

He glanced around the small townhouse. The only Christmas decoration was the tree by the window.

Good, he thought, *blocks the view from the outside.*

He reached into his back pants pocket and pulled out a pair of leather gloves. Small, red stains still showed in between the fingers on one glove. Glenn examined the stains for a moment and picked at it with his fingernail. After this, he'd have to carefully dab them clean. These were nice gloves. Italian leather. No reason to let them just stain and ruin.

Jenny's place was bare. She didn't have pictures of herself, friends, or her parents. Not even a pet. His previous loners at least had pictures of their pets.

Jennifer Pearl was a sad sack for sure. All he needed was a cute dog and a smile, and she was dying to drop her pants for him. He almost felt sorry for her, but why waste the emotion. No one would miss her. Hell, with it being as cold as it was, her body wouldn't stink for a month. And really, how many people actually visited the library often enough to realize something was wrong?

Glenn slithered through the living room and into the kitchen. A set of kitchen knives were neatly displayed in their block on the counter. He doubted she'd ever used the knives. Probably ordered takeout for every meal. It was time to put one of them to good use. Well, one to start with. When the carving began, he might spread the love around, just so some of the other knives could feel useful.

"You can come back whenever you're ready. Have a present you can unwrap," she hollered.

Glenn rolled his eyes at the Christmas joke. What was it with this town and Christmas?

He could practically hear the desire dripping from her voice. He slid the gloves onto his hands and grabbed the chef's knife out of the block. The OJ Simpson special. It pulled away with ease. The pristine edge and sleek silver glistened in the light. He smiled at his reflection in the knife's blade.

"I can't wait to unwrap my present," he said, still admiring his own image.

Slowly, he lowered the knife and stepped down the hall. The door was left slightly ajar, a sliver of light cascaded from the bedroom into the hallway. He gently brushed his free hand against the door, letting it naturally swing open.

His smile slowly dripped from his face as he saw the bed was empty. He'd expected her to be there waiting for him. As he stepped into the room, he briefly saw the bat swing at his head before his vision doubled. He was unconscious before his body hit the floor.

He'd never felt pain at this level before. Every thought hurt. From somewhere close by, he heard a television. The noise repeatedly stabbed into his scalp like an ice pick.

Finally, he forced his eyes to open, despite the excruciating pain. Slowly, his vision cleared.

He was strapped to a chair with zip ties. His arms were bound at his wrists and just before his elbows. His legs were also zip tied at his ankles and just below his knees. A television sat in front of him. He couldn't tell what was on. His vision hadn't cleared that much yet. The walls were covered in carpet and soundproofing material. Aside from the television, a single light bulb provided the only illumination.

"Where..." he tried to say but couldn't. His lips wouldn't part. They were stuck together. Any attempt to separate them shot rays of pain across his face.

"Where are you?" Jenny finished the question for him. She turned down the television's volume. "You're in my basement, sweetie."

"How?" Again, needles of pain plastered his mouth.

"I hit you in the head with a baseball bat. I'm so glad you have a thick skull. I was worried that was going to split your head wide open."

Jenny grabbed a chair and pulled it across the floor. A loud screech screamed throughout the basement, and

Glenn whimpered from the pain. She stopped the chair in front of him and sat down.

"I recognized you almost immediately. It was the dimples that gave you away. Sure, you can dye your hair, but those dimples." She shook her head. "I'm a huge fan of your work. Really am. The shock I had when an artist like yourself showed up in this little town. It was all I could do to keep from geeking out right then. Your work in New York...beautiful. Oh, and the girl in Rhode Island, I mean, she was a perfect canvas for you."

Glenn tried to process what she was saying. Before he could start, she kept on.

"I'm very honored that you wanted to make me your next victim. Truly, I am. You should feel equally as honored, because you're going to be mine."

From under his chair, she grabbed the knife that he had planned to kill her with. She held it by the handle and flashed the blade his direction. For a brief moment, but just long enough, he saw his reflection and why he couldn't open his mouth. She'd sown his mouth shut. Criss crossed red and green stitching laced his lips together.

Once she knew he'd seen his reflection, she shoved the knife into his thigh and pulled it out. She then did it again to the other thigh.

Glenn's eyes spread wide open. He screamed behind the sown-together lips. His hands shook against their restraints.

"This isn't my first time. If I tie it at the wrists and elbows and at the ankles and knees, you're pretty much unable to move at all. I also know exactly where to cut to make it hurt but not kill. If you're lucky, I might even take a stitch or two out." She pointed the knife at his mouth.

Glenn flared his nostrils trying to breathe through his nose rapidly.

"I've missed having someone to spend the holidays with. I'm really, really grateful that you came into my life when you did. Do you know how lonely Christmas in Hallmark can be?" She smiled at him, and he stared into her eyes. Eyes that were dark beyond darkness. Whatever soul should've been in those eyes was long gone.

"We're going to spend the whole season together. We can watch the candlelight ceremony, the cookie competition, all of it. Just you and me. Oh, and Cooper. He's upstairs eating. Such a cute boy. Anyway, I have a ton of the best Christmas movies queued up for us to watch. All based on stories from right here in our little town. Are you ready for a Hallmark Christmas Movie Marathon?"

Santa's Roadside Assistant

B ryce Campbell gripped the steering wheel as the snowfall increased. He resisted the urge to lift his foot off the gas. Slowing down was the last thing he wanted to do. He had his eyes set on Montreal. A stupid snowstorm in Middle of Nowhere, Vermont wasn't about to stop him.

As much as he didn't want to admit it, Bryce should've listened to his mother.

"Bryce," she had said the last time he called. "Just fly up to Montreal for the holidays. It'll be so much easier and quicker than if you drove."

"My Mustang never gets out of the parking garage, Mom," he had told her. "I've barely driven the damn thing since I moved to the city."

"It's going to snow," she had warned.

"I know, Mom. I've been driving in snow since I was five."

"Yeah, but you've been in New York City so long, taking taxis or the subway to that job of yours, you probably forgot how. What kind of son leaves the comfort and protection of his sweet mother's house to work in such a big place where no one knows your name? And just so you can play with other people's money."

"Mom, I don't play with other people's money. I'm a stockbroker. I make a good living, and I enjoy what I do."

This, he thought. *This is why I don't call very often, and this is why I never come to visit.*

If it wasn't for the holidays, he would've found an excuse not to go. But it was Christmas. Well, to be exact, it was a week before Christmas. Yes, he knew he should've flown, but then he'd have been stuck at his mother's, without a vehicle, unable to escape whenever he needed. He could've rented a car, but that would've been just another argument. "Why rent a car? I can pick you up from the airport and take you back."

Her voice grated on his last nerve.

Driving, despite being stuck in a goddamn snowstorm, was the better choice. Plus, it made transporting the presents for his nephews easier. They were the only reason he was making the trip, really.

Not because of his mother, but because he missed those two boys. His sister was slowly bleeding the manhood out of them just like she had her ex-husband. Bryce hoped to be a good masculine influence on their lives and counterbalance his sister who was hell bent on neutering them. Come hell or high water, he was going to show them what it meant to actually be a man.

He passed a sign for the next town. It read "Hallmark 5mi". That sounded like a great name for a town. Hopefully, he'd be able to find a place to stop, take a piss, fill up with gas, grab a bite to eat, then continue on the road. It was almost eight, and he still had four more hours to go. Well, four hours in good weather. Bryce hoped the snowfall would ease up just enough to let him drive the speed he wanted.

The Mustang's headlights reflected off the stark white snow. Bryce struggled to see the road ahead. Large maple trees hugged the sides and extended into the night sky. All Bryce could see was darkness, trees, and snow.

Silence filled the car. Bryce realized the Christmas music playlist he had on as background noise had ended. Thinking about the conversation with his mother, he hadn't even noticed. He reached for his phone, momentarily taking his eyes off the road. He unlocked it, swiped up, and opened his music app. He clicked play on another Christmas playlist and glanced up just in time.

Large doe eyes stared at him from the middle of the road, and he was barreling straight for them. The deer stood, hypnotized by the two headlights. Its black eyes seemed to peer through the windshield and straight into Bryce's soul.

"Shit!" he screamed and slammed on the brakes as hard as he could, forcing the pedal all the way against the floorboard. He yanked the steering wheel to the right, hoping the Mustang reacted in time to avoid hitting the deer.

The tires locked. The car skidded. The smell of burnt rubber engulfed the area. Time slowed, and Bryce was painfully aware of every detail. Fortunately, the tires found some traction and reengaged with the road, inches from hitting the deer, sending his car careening toward the side of the road. He suddenly stopped in a small ditch just beyond the pavement.

Bryce's head hit the steering wheel and ricocheted back against the seat's headrest. He sat there, dazed. His heart raced, and he struggled to catch his breath. He smelled burnt rubber from the tires. His hand went to his forehead. At the slightest touch, he winced from the sharp pain. A glance in his rearview mirror showed the goose egg already forming.

After sitting for a few minutes, letting adrenaline slowly drain from his system, he placed his hand on the key and turned the ignition. The car tried to turnover, but then something metallic rattled ominously within the engine and it died. Steam began to billow out from under the hood.

"No, no, no," he said.

He pulled on the hood release, and a steam cloud escaped from the engine. Bryce opened the door and jumped out of the car. A sudden wave of dizziness knocked him back, forcing him to brace against the car door. Too much quick movement after a head injury apparently.

Keeping one hand on the car, he shuffled to the front. Snow fell all around, resting on top of the Mustang. The damp cold bit into his hands. His numbing fingers searched for the latch to free the hood. After a few frustrating seconds, he found it. As he raised it all the way, the remaining steam hit him squarely in the face, temporarily blinding him.

Bryce stared into the engine block but had absolutely no idea what he was searching for. He had no knowledge about cars. It was never something he had found interesting. He was beginning to regret that.

He slammed the hood closed and marched to the driver's side. He opened the door and flopped down behind the wheel again. His mother's words floated back to the front of his brain. There was no telling how much grief he was going to get now.

He grasped the cellphone sitting in the seat next to him and pulled up his insurance company's app. He clicked through the prompts for roadside assistance. Within seconds, a truck had been dispatched to his location. He was looking for Moonlight Towing.

"Fitting name," Bryce said. "Moon's the only light in the sky."

He closed the car door, hoping to maintain whatever heat he could, and rested his head against the headrest. He closed his eyes and waited.

Twenty minutes later, bright, flashing lights lit up the entire area. Snow had piled on top of the car's hood, creating a white blanket over the red Mustang's top. The tow truck's lights immediately blinded Bryce's eyes, and he squinted away from their harsh beams. Beyond the rumble of the truck's engine, he heard a door open and slam shut. Soon a silhouetted figure knocked on his window.

He pulled on the door handle, swinging it open. He shivered as the cold air rushed in. As he rose out of the driver's seat, his eyes finally adjusted to the light.

He had expected an overweight, bearded man in stained overalls, smelling of cigarettes and booze. Instead, he saw the most strikingly beautiful woman. She had straight black hair and deep red lipstick. Her skin was as white as the falling snow. She had eyes as green as emeralds that captured the truck's lights, sparkling back as if they were precious stones. She wore overalls that hung relatively loose on her, which only added to the mystique. Bryce couldn't quite make out how lovely her curves were, leaving an air of mystery.

"I'm guessing you're Mr. Campbell," she said, glancing down at her tablet before raising her eyes back to his. Her voice had a low, seductive quality about it.

He was so captivated, and for a moment he forgot who he was. After an awkward pause, he stuttered out, "Camp...Campbell? Campbell. Yes, that's me. You can call me Bryce." He held his hand out.

She grasped it and squeezed. Bryce was amazed at the strength of her grip, but also the softness of her skin. She withdrew her hand and pointed to the car. "Looks like you had a little incident. It's not starting up?"

"No, it died. Steam poured out from the hood when I tried to start it."

"Probably damaged the radiator. Well, let's get it up on the truck. You got a ride that can come pick you up?"

She didn't wait for a response. Instead, she turned and went back to the truck, reached into her back pocket, and pulled out a pair of gloves.

"No. I'm just driving through. Family is another five hours away. At least."

"Well, I hope you aren't in a rush," she said, her voice pulling him toward her as she moved further away. "Shop's not open until Monday. And with it being the holidays, getting parts is going to be tough. Good thing for you, though, Hallmark is a great town for the holidays. Plenty of festivities over the next couple of days to keep you entertained."

"Couple of days? You think I'll be stuck here for a few days?"

"Quite possibly."

Bryce had an idea and funneled up some of his boyish charm that had won him his job at the brokerage firm. "I guess it wouldn't be too bad to stick around for a few days. Maybe you could show me around... what's the name of this town again?"

"Hallmark," she answered. She reached the truck and turned back to him. "I need to get your car on the truck. Stand over there and let me get you loaded up. While I'm taking you into town, we can talk about the rest."

Bryce smiled. "What's your name, by the way?" he hollered while moving to the other side of the road.

"Yvonne," she answered as she hopped into the truck.

Bryce was impressed with how quickly she got his Mustang onto the bed of the tow truck. She moved with such grace and skill. He had barely realized what was happening before the car was secured and ready.

"You getting in?" she asked.

Without answering, he grabbed the passenger door handle, yanked it open, and hopped inside. The truck was spotless. There were no abandoned takeout wrappers or empty drink cups. The dash was as dust-free as if it had just been cleaned that evening. However, there was an overwhelming smell of sweet lavender.

Yvonne pulled herself up behind the steering wheel. She glanced at Bryce. Was it his imagination or did her eyes seem to linger?

Is she checking me out?

"So, this town of yours likes celebrating Christmas?" he asked, trying to drum up conversation. "I'm a huge fan of Christmas. Have some presents for my nephews in the car. Holidays are always special. The decorations, the music. I even love all those cheesy, cliche Christmas movies on the Hallmark Channel. What about you?"

She trailed her fingers behind her ears, brushing her long black hair away from her face. She smiled, spreading her red lips from one side of her face to the other. "Oh, the movies are the best."

She turned her body and faced him as the truck idled in park only a few feet from where his car had crashed into the embankment.

He continued. "I know they're always so predictable, but when you add in that little spark of Christmas magic, well, who can resist?" He adjusted his body to face her, raising his knee onto the seat and scooting a bit closer.

She leaned in. "Tell me if you've seen this one. So, there's a cute guy who's coming from the big city."

"You're going to have to give me more than that. There's a couple hundred of them."

She laughed, "Take it easy. I'm not done."

Yvonne cleared her throat and scooted closer. "This guy is coming from the big city. He's driving through that typical small town but gets stuck. Car breaks down, and he isn't able to leave for a few days. A townsperson directs him to a local inn where the innkeeper is an attractive, single woman. It's also the only place in town with no Christmas lights, because the innkeeper hates Christmas."

Bryce slid a little closer, smiling and chuckling as she relayed the plot of at least a dozen Hallmark Christmas movies. His knee bumped into hers. He left it there, slightly touching, hoping she felt the same spark of energy. Since she hadn't moved her leg or started driving away, he thought she might be into him as well.

"This movie does sound familiar," he said, nodding his head. "I do think I saw those."

"So he asks her why she doesn't like Christmas, and she gives a sappy backstory about how she'd been wronged before by some heartless guy, and ever since, well, she just doesn't have the holiday spirit. He makes it his mission, while he's stuck there in that little town, to show her the true meaning of Christmas." Her hand rubbed the side of her leg and rested millimeters from his knee.

"You know," Bryce started. "I can see some similarities to that movie and what's happened here. I'm a cute guy from a big city. I'm stuck due to some car trouble. Is there a cute innkeeper in town that needs to know the true meaning of Christmas?" Leaning closer and resting his hand on her leg, he asked, "Or maybe a very beautiful tow truck driver? Santa's roadside assistant?"

"You're partly right," Yvonne said, placing her own hand on top of his. "The beginning of that movie does sound familiar."

Bryce felt pressure and pain. When he glanced down, she gripped his hand extremely tight. Tight enough that his knuckles ground together. "Wow, you have a very strong grip." He tried not to grimace.

She maintained a wide smile across her face. Her emerald eyes drilled holes into him. "It is like what's happened here. Hallmark is great like that. Real life mimicking those cliche Christmas movies. But the ending of our movie...oh, it's going to be so. Much. Better."

Her grip intensified. Sharp nails Bryce hadn't noticed before pierced his hand, and droplets of blood fell onto the leg of her overalls.

He shifted off the bench seat, falling onto the floorboard, trying to pry his hand back. "I'm sorry for touching your leg! I thought we were clicking. Fuck! Ow!"

"The way our movie will end..." she started. As she did, her voice changed. It went from her low, seductive tone to something deep and coarse. The same tone that someone working in sound effects would give a character possessed by a demon. Barely human. "...it ends with your blood splattered across the cab of my tow truck."

Her unusually long, sharp nails buried into his hand, tearing through tendons and crushing bones. Her other hand shot out and gripped him around the throat. With ease, she lifted him off the floorboard and pinned his head against the roof of the truck's cab.

Pain ripped through his entire arm. He wanted to cry out, but her grip on his neck was too tight. Instead his mouth hung open in a silent scream, and his eyes opened wide with terror. This beautiful tow truck driver had pulverized his hand and suspended him in the air. Nothing made sense.

Trembling, he stared down at her. As he did, her lips separated. Her stark white teeth appeared too large for her mouth, and each one had a sharp point at the end.

Bryce gripped the arm holding him in the air with his free hand, but instead of the soft, smooth skin he'd felt earlier, her flesh was rough. Long, coarse black hair rapidly spread across her arm. Bryce's hand became engulfed by thick fur.

Yvonne's face contorted. Her mouth and oversized fangs elongated outwards, pulling away from her cheeks. They morphed into a snout like a dog or a wolf. Her ears grew and sharpened to a point. The same black fur that covered her arm spread across her neck and face.

Somewhere in his fracturing psyche, he realized what was going on. His beautiful tow truck driver, his savior in the snow, Santa's roadside assistant, was a fucking were-wolf.

Panicked, he hit her arm with his free hand and attempted to kick her, but inside the confines of the truck, his legs harmlessly glanced off her.

She lowered her arm, bringing his face close to hers. Inches away, she let out an ear-piercing roar.

The stench of death and animal overpowered the lavender that had filled the cab. *No wonder she used so much air freshener*, he thought. Her claws pierced into the side of his neck. Thick, warm blood flowed down his shirt. It pooled onto the bench seat.

One last thought came before darkness overtook him.

I should've flown to Montreal.

Yvonne finally let go of Bryce's mutilated hand and wrapped her arm completely around his torso.

Bryce felt tension on his shoulders and neck as he stared into her emerald eyes. Every tendon, muscle, and joint pulled to its capacity. Searing pain ripped through his neck as the skin just below his Adam's apple separated. Blood gushed out as the tear spread, exposing his arteries and esophagus.

Fortunately for Bryce, the darkness came just before she finished pulling his head from his shoulders.

Yvonne dabbed at her mouth with a napkin, cleaning off the last of her nighttime snack.

Once she finished feasting on her raw New York City steak, she shoved the remains inside the Mustang and drove to Lake Providence, just outside of Hallmark. She backed the truck up to the bank, unhooked the Mustang, and placed the car in neutral. Once the bed of the truck was angled down, she delivered one inhumanly strong push and sent the red sports car and all its contents into the lake.

Yvonne hung out next to the truck, waiting and watching as the car slowly sunk into the dark waters.

Once the last of the air bubbles subsided, she strode back to the driver's door. Blood, intestines, and gore covered the interior of her truck. As soon as she got back to the office, she'd have to wash it out. Again.

Driving back to Hallmark, she glanced at the full moon and rested her hand on her full belly. She loved holiday travelers.

Gingerbread Cookie
Throwdown

"Ladies and Gentlemen, welcome to the Forty-Fifth Annual Gingerbread Cookie Throwdown!" Jerry Stanley, the local TV news anchor, announced into the microphone.

The stage was set in the center of Hallmark with the picturesque courthouse towering behind it. Twelve temporary cooking stations lined the stage. In between every other station was a double oven. The odd numbered stations used the top oven, and the even numbered stations used the bottom one. Each station was the same size, the same shape, and equipped with the same instruments: cookie cutters, piping bags, ingredients, food coloring, and measuring cups. Everything that a kitchen needed to make the perfect gingerbread cookie.

The twelve contestants stood shoulder to shoulder across the front of the stage. Each one wore a holiday sweater, a red or green dress, and a Santa hat or elf ears. Hair pristinely done and not a strand out of place. Makeup perfectly applied for the lights and television cameras. No one wanted to look bad when all of Hallmark was watching.

"Although I don't think we have any newcomers in the audience," Jerry continued, "I'll still read through the rules. First, you can only use the ingredients at your station. No sneaking in a little something extra. Betty, I'm looking at you." He pointed to the row of contestants.

The fourth lady down feigned embarrassment and shook her head. The two next to her politely touched her shoulder and laughed along with her.

"Second, make as many gingerbread cookies as you want.

"Third, your cookies must be decorated. A plain gingerbread cookie... well, that's just a travesty, am I right?" He turned to the audience and was greeted with resounding applause.

"And lastly and most importantly, remember the reason for the season. This Throwdown is all in good fun. Your toy and food donations will go to those less fortunate, so they can also enjoy the holiday spirit that is always so overwhelmingly special here in Hallmark."

A chorus of "aaahhh"'s came from the crowd.

"One last thing before we get started. Let's meet our judges, shall we?" Jerry Stanley turned to the table set up on stage right. "We have three with us today. You know two of them. We have our wonderful mayor, and my little brother, Bob Stanley."

Bob, who'd just turned fifty, stood in his blue jeans and green Grinch sweater. He waved to the audience.

"Next to him, you know her as my co-anchor and the weather girl on WHMM Channel Eight, Stephanie Lori."

The attractive brunette to the mayor's left stood up. She wore red leggings and a white sweater with Santa's face on it. The caption read "100% Chance of Presents". She also waved to the crowd.

"And rounding out our judging panel, we have a newcomer visiting us from Montpelier. From the Times Argus Newspaper, give a warm Hallmark welcome to Carol O'Bannon."

An older woman with short gray hair and black cat-eyed glasses stood up. She was dressed in a long green dress over a white long-sleeved shirt. A black, knitted Christmas vest draped across her thin frame. She looked as if a slight breeze might carry her away. She gently nodded as the crowd gave a lackluster applause.

"Well, let's see," Jerry said, "We've gone over the rules. We've met our judges. What's left for us to do?"

"Start baking!" the crowd yelled back to him in unison.

"What was that?" He put his hand up to his ear, egging on the swarm of onlookers.

"Start baking!"

"Well, ladies, you heard them. Step up to your stations." The twelve contestants marched over to their appropriate tables and started organizing supplies. "Judges, please put twenty minutes on the clock."

Mayor Bob pressed a button on the control panel in front of him. A large digital stopwatch above the judges' head lit up with "20:00".

Jerry Stanley stood in the center of the stage. He gazed from one side to the other, verifying each contestant was ready to go. Once his head made the trek from station one to station twelve, he turned back around to the patiently awaiting audience.

"Ladies."

The crowd leaned in.

"Start. Your. Baking!" He elongated the last syllable, letting the word ring out over the entire courtyard.

"Look who it is," Jackie said, pointing just past the stage. She stood in the crowd as the clock ticked down.

She enjoyed the Cookie Throwdown. Anyone could win. It really just depended on how the cookie crumbled, as they say.

"I can't tell from here," Evelyn said, squinting in the direction Jackie pointed.

They'd grown up together. Both were twenty-three years old, had graduated the same year from Hallmark High, and even participated on the cheer squad together ("Go, Devils").

"He's the only one who couldn't care less about all of this," she said.

The older man sauntered three blocks away with his head down and hands in his pocket. Jackie didn't need to see his face to know he was scowling. She'd seen it enough growing up.

"Oh, that's Mr. Richards," Evelyn answered. "What's he doing downtown this time of year? I thought as soon as decorations went up, he stayed away from here."

"He does. Old man must've gotten lost or something. Wouldn't surprise me. He's weird. I've seen him muttering to himself while walking down the sidewalk. He lives in that huge house all alone."

"It's the only house on the block, hell, the whole town, without lights. Can you imagine the Christmas light show you could have in a house like that? Criminal really," Evelyn said.

"How much time is left on the clock?" Jackie asked.

Evelyn craned her neck to the judges' table. "Fifteen minutes. Won't be long before the first competitors come out of the oven." She paced back and forth, clutching her arms across her chest.

"You cold, Evelyn?" Jackie asked, mockingly.

"Shut up, Jackie, it's cold just standing around. Hey, speaking of standing around, look at the back of the crowd."

As Jackie started to turn, Evelyn grabbed her and kept her from turning. "No, don't turn around," she said.

"Then, how am I supposed to see what's back there?" Jackie asked, frustrated with Evelyn.

"Not what. Who." Evelyn said the last of it with a grin across her face.

"Oh Lord, Evelyn. I know that look. There's only one person you've ever given that look for." Jackie broke free of Evelyn's grip and turned. "I knew it. Brett Stephens. You are too predictable, and by the look of it, you're still crushing on him. How long has it been since you last saw him? Four years?"

"We broke up two weeks after graduation."

"Oh, I remember," Jackie said, nodding her head and rolling her eyes. "Four long years since the football star on his way to the big leagues dumped the cheer leader who insisted on staying in Hallmark."

"You don't have to sound so happy about it." Evelyn rolled her eyes at Jackie in return.

"Well, I'd say you could go say hi to him, but it looks like he's with someone." Jackie tried to hold back a snicker but a little one escaped.

"You're a bitch sometimes, you know," Evelyn said, pouting. "She isn't even his type."

"Hmmm, let's see. Obviously store bought blond hair, nice tits, and a flat stomach. Yeah. She's really no one's type."

Evelyn turned back to the competition.

"The first gingerbread men are coming out," Evelyn said. There was no more playfulness in her tone.

"Ladies, we have ten minutes left on the clock," Jerry Stanley announced. "Ten minutes to get your gingerbread men out of the oven and decorated. We wouldn't want any faceless gingerbread men. You remember what happened last time."

"Last time?" Carol O'Bannon asked Stephanie the Weather Girl.

"Just watch. The Throwdown is *really* about to start," Stephanie replied.

"Didn't it start ten minutes ago?"

"That was just the baking portion."

"I..." Carol started. She was at a loss for words. What Stephanie said in a way made sense. Yes, the contestants had to bake the gingerbread men before they could decorate them, but the baking competition started ten...now eleven...minutes ago. In her opinion, the prepping and baking were critical components. "I guess you're right, Ms. Lori. It's just an odd way of describing it."

"Hey, Bob," Stephanie said, tapping him on the shoulder. When he turned his head, she continued, "Who do you think is going to win it all this year?"

"Ooohh, well, from what I could see of the trays, most went fairly traditional. With the amount of dough available, those have five men and a few accessories. Pretty typical. Station eight had an interesting take. Hers appear to be smaller and thinner. I think she's going for numbers over brute strength. Station eleven went the opposite route, though. She used all her dough and made one big gingerbread man; nothing there to fight with. I don't think I've ever seen that strategy before."

"Oh, come on, Bob, you didn't give me a straight answer," Stephanie prodded. "Give me a number. Who are you thinking?"

He took a deep breath and audibly sighed. "If you want to hold me to a number, I'm going to go with..."

His eyes danced from station to station. With the ladies concentrating on decorating their men, he could only see so much of what they had.

"I'm going to go with six. She made smaller stars, so more of them. And a few with some really tight edges."

"I like eight and her mini gingerbread men. I think she's got the winning strategy," Stephanie said. She turned to Carol and leaned back so the reporter could participate in the conversation. "Carol, what are your thoughts?"

Carol's face showed everything she thought. Her forehead scrunched together in confusion. "What do tight edges or accessories have to do with gingerbread cookies?" She took a deep breath and huffed it out. Frustrated, she continued. "What does any of what you two are saying have to do with baking? I've judged a lot of cooking and baking competitions all across New England. How are the cookies decorated? How do they taste? What's their texture and aroma? Those are the parts of a typical scoring rubric for a cookie competition."

Stephanie kept her smile on her face. "Texture? Aroma? Well, if you want to get that close, you can, but I wouldn't recommend it. And taste? Well, those are just fighting words," she said and laughed at her own joke.

Stephanie turned her attention back to Bob, leaving Carol more confused than she already was.

Each contestant had their cookies out of the oven and on the table with the exception of station eleven. Station eleven patiently waited for her one really big gingerbread cookie to finish baking while the other ladies all held piping bags in their hands, delicately decorating their cookies. Carol didn't know why eleven would want to do one really big one. She ran the risk of it being crunchy and dried out on the outside and possibly not done on the inside.

"Contestants, you have five minutes remaining. Only five more minutes to have your cookies ready for the Gingerbread Cookie Throwdown." Jerry's voice boomed from the speakers. He turned his attention offstage. "Gentleman, let's get started."

"Get started?" Carol asked her fellow judges. "Get started with what?"

"The Throwdown. Aren't you paying attention?" Stephanie answered. Her tone said she was starting to worry about Carol's cognitive abilities.

From offstage, a group of stagehands carried large fence panels. They sat the fence panels down in the center of the stage and stood them up. Each panel of fencing was a three-foot-by-three-foot square. Stagehands used clamps to bind them together. Eight panels formed an octagon. Once all eight were standing and clamped together, they secured the structure to the stage. Finally, an octagon-shaped panel was carried in and placed just outside of the arena.

A few cameras were brought in and positioned around the cage. As the stagehands turned them on, two giant TV screens which flanked the stage came to life. The image showed the empty octagon.

"Two minutes, contestants. Two minutes."

Carol glanced at contestant eleven. She slid her sheet pan out of the oven and sat it in front of her. Having baked all her life, Carol knew eleven didn't have any time remaining to decorate her cookie with any kind of detail. Plus, it was still hot. Any icing she'd put on it would start to melt. Despite the lack of time, Eleven held the piping bag in her hand and dabbed icing across her one large cookie.

"One minute before piping bags down."

With a look at the audience, Carol saw their faces glued to the stage. Everyone waited with bated breath, staring at the clock. The contestants moved their hands with delicate precision, hoping to get those last bits of detail put on that would hopefully give them the edge.

"Ten, nine, eight," Jerry Stanley said into the microphone. The crowd and Carol's fellow judges joined in.

"Seven, six, five."

The contestants furiously moved their hands over their trays.

"Four, three, two, one. Bags down, ladies."

All twelve sat their bags down, put their hands up, and stepped away from their tables. Despite the cold weather, sweat glistened on their foreheads. Smiling, they glanced at each other. A few distributed hugs to their competition.

"Great job, contestants."

Carol found herself anxious to try the cookies. Gingerbread was her favorite. She decided to ignore the odd discussion of her counterparts and just do what she was called here to do. Judge Hallmark's Forty-Fifth Annual Gingerbread Cookie Throwdown.

"Now's the time you've all been waiting for. Gentleman, the trays."

The stagehands who had built the octagon returned. The six men grabbed two trays each and carried them to the octagon. The poor stagehand who was tasked with contestants Eleven and Twelve seemed to struggle with the centralized weight of the one large gingerbread man.

Carol, confused, glanced at Stephanie and Bob. Each of them leaned forward, eyes wide, like they were ready to watch a spectacle. Why weren't the men bringing the cookies to the judges' table for viewing?

The men reached over the tops of the panels and set the trays down inside the octagon. They ran to grab the eight-sided panel and carried it over, gently setting it down on top of the structure and securing it with more clamps, effectively sealing the gingerbread cookies inside.

"Contestants, audience members, and those watching at home." Jerry gave an exaggerated pause. "It's time for..." He took a big breath before belting out, "THE THROW-DOWN!"

Carol turned and peered at the octagon. What the hell were they waiting on? Then, suddenly, she got her answer.

One small gingerbread arm rose off a pan.

Gingerbread man after gingerbread man peeled themselves from the trays. When one stood up, it stumbled over to another cookie on the same tray, one that hadn't fully risen yet, and used its flat, handless arm to assist. The arm slid under its friend's back like a spatula and assisted its teammate upright.

Others, instead of helping their fellow tray mates, slid their arms under the baked instruments on their tray. They grasped little pieces of dough rolled and baked in the shape of daggers, swords, or stars and held them high.

The icing on the cookies moved with the cookies themselves. Their mouths smiled and then puckered.

Most trays held only five or six gingerbread men. Tray Eight, with its short, skinny cookies, had a dozen standing ready, and each clutched a tiny sword.

Tray Eleven, with its one large gingerbread cookie, remained still. The icing had melted, streaking across its face. Its eyes had almost melted completely away, leaving a jagged, open, unfocused stare. Carol knew if she could've gazed into that stare, she would've seen the depths of... She shivered and tried to focus on anything else.

The gingerbread men huddled together in the center of their respective trays and began planning. Occasionally, they glanced at tray eleven, but he still hadn't shown any signs of life.

The crowd waited anxiously for the fight to begin. Twelve factions - well, eleven since Eleven hadn't moved - all strategizing on how best to attack their foes.

Although the crowd was excited, Carol watched in horror. What kind of madness?

Maybe it's some kind of CGI?

"Does the fence have a screen inside of it? One that created the special effects?" Carol asked Stephanie and Bob.

Both of them glared at her, as if they blamed her ignorance for the current situation.

"Special effects?" Bob asked. "What special effects?"

"The gingerbread men!" she nearly screamed.

"What about them?" he asked in return.

"Would you two be quiet?" Stephanie interrupted. "They just broke their huddles. Too bad about Eleven. Would've loved to see the big guy."

As Stephanie spoke, the various groups broke from their huddles and took up positions around their trays. Each stood their ground, as if the tray was their home base and no invading army was going to take it. Capture the Flag. But deadly. With gingerbread men.

The first cookies broke from their trays and attacked their neighbors. A dozen fights broke out. They stabbed with their cookie swords and daggers. Stars acted as shields, blocking attacks. Tray Eight had double the number of fighters. In pairs, they slowly chopped pieces of their opponent away until a leg finally snapped. The gingerbread leg broke apart from the body, and its owner tumbled to the ground. Three of Tray Eight's men jumped onto the fallen soldier and pummeled him into cookie dust.

The tides swayed back and forth. Tray One's soldiers advanced on Tray Two and made great advances, but then Tray Four joined up with Tray Two and fought them back. Tray Eight's swarm attack continued to work well until Tray Six and Seven teamed up and overpowered the smaller cookies.

Chunks of gingerbread covered the ground. Crumbled pieces were soon stomped into dust beneath the feet of the victors.

The entire scene was cookie mayhem until a low rumble broke out. The few dozen left still in the fight immediately halted their attacks.

Even the crowd held its breath.

From inside the cage, a deep moan shook the octagon. The gingerbread men, some missing an arm, others with cracks, visibly shook in fear. From Tray Eleven, a large arm rose into the air. It slammed back down onto the ground, shaking the stage. The other arm rose from the tray, reached for the top of the cage, and then slammed down onto the ground as well. With both arms free, the giant pressed down, and slowly rose its head and torso.

The icing on the face was disfigured. One eye was nothing more than a streak across the side of its face. The other had shifted into the middle of its forehead, like a mutilated cyclops. The mouth had slipped almost to the neck, making it appear grotesquely too large for its face.

The gingerbread monster rose up onto its two legs. Wobbly at first, it grasped the fence and steadied itself. Standing upright, it towered over all the other men. Its head ended less than an inch from the top of the octagon.

With its one good eye, it stared down at the gingerbread men below it, leaned its head down, and roared.

The audience, the judges, and even Jerry Stanley gasped at the newly awakened cookie monster.

Jerry, who'd been relatively quiet during the tiny fights within the octagon, finally chimed in. "Ladies and Gentleman, I believe we are in for a treat now. The Goliath of Tray Eleven has awoken. Will the surviving men band together to defeat him? Let's watch."

No sooner had he said those words than the remaining soldiers, close to three dozen, charged at Goliath. With a kick of its leg, Goliath sent the first three into the fence. They shattered against the side, sending cookie fragments through the wires and across the stage.

A few others made it close enough to start stabbing Goliath's feet and legs. Some maneuvered around to its back and tried from behind. Tray Eight's remaining men climbed the side of the fence and jumped onto Goliath's back and head.

The beast swung its arms from side to side and kicked its feet. Occasionally, it connected with one of the smaller cookies, kicking them away from him. Once, he stomped down so hard, he crushed two of the other soldiers.

Thrashing his arms, he collided with the fence. The whole octagon shook. Goliath must've realized his effect.

Ignoring the inconsequential attacks of the other ginger-bread men, Goliath pounded on the fence. With each massive blow, the fence shook, and a gap between neighboring panels widened. The clamps began to spread open, not rated for a gingerbread man the size of Goliath.

After creating a large enough separation, Goliath took a few steps back and ran at the loosened fence. It gave way and crashed onto the ground.

He let out a roar; King Kong escaping from his cage.

Sensing freedom, the remaining gingerbread men rushed out of the octagon. A dozen of them swarmed the judges' table and jumped onto Carol, Stephanie, and Bob. Jerry went to help his brother, but a few hopped on the announcer and used their cookie swords to stab him. They grabbed his tie and wrangled him to the ground.

The crowd screamed and ran as the gingerbread men hopped off the stage and into the audience.

Goliath hobbled over to Station Eleven. The lady who'd created him bent down and picked him up, cradling him in her arms.

"Mom-ma," Goliath said.

With a tear in her eye and a smile across her face, she nodded.

Goliath raised his hand, which held a knife from his mother's station. "Mom-ma," he said again, and then buried the knife into her neck.

Arterial blood spurted out as she fell to her knees.

All around, gingerbread men wreaked havoc, toppling the cameras, the tables, and the chairs. People ran away screaming as gingerbread men clung to their hair, their necks, and their legs.

At the judges' table, Mayor Bob Stanley and weather girl Stephanie Lori had escaped, but Carol O'Bannon lay face down, a widening pool of blood spreading across the table in front of her.

No place more
special

"Your father's will contained specific instructions regarding how you should handle his estate after his passing." Wilton Johnson said.

The elderly attorney sat behind his diminutive desk. Stacks of manila folders, overflowing with paperwork, covered the filing cabinets behind him. Every time he moved in his metal swivel chair, an ear-piercing creak accompanied it.

This was not how Harper Reed had expected to spend her holidays. She'd spent most of her young adult life trying to get out of Hallmark. Now, here she was, a nice apartment in Manhattan, her dream job working for Vogue, and enjoying life to its fullest. No dog. No kids. No boyfriend. Just Harper.

"How long do I have to stay here before all of this is wrapped up?" she asked.

"Well, with Christmas around the corner, a lot of people are on vacation." He picked up her father's will, his eyes shifting back and forth behind his glasses as he read through it again. "His ashes have already been taken care of, so you don't need to worry with that. But the estate sale won't occur until the new year. It stipulates in his will you have to stay here in Hallmark until it's complete."

"And if I don't? You knew my father. Is it that big of a deal I live my own life away from here?"

Harper's frustration flowed out of her. Sure, she could work remotely. That wasn't the issue. She hated this town. Hated all the stupid holiday traditions. The last thing she wanted was to be stuck in the house she'd grown up in for the next two or three weeks. Especially now.

"It expressly states you must stay there." Wilton glanced up from the will, placed it on his desk, and leaned forward. The chair cried as it moved. "Your father hated it when you moved away."

"I'm aware. He made that abundantly obvious." She crossed her arms and rolled her eyes.

"If I was a betting man, I would guess he put that in here because he knew it would be the only way you'd stay for any length of time. So hopefully you'd find that spark of joy here and want to stay.

"Your father loved this town. Loved the magic it possessed, especially during the Christmas season. 'No place is more special than Hallmark,' he always said. 'Except...'"

"'Except for Disney World.' Yes, I heard it a million times." Harper uncrossed her arms and held them in her lap. "All I have to do is stay here for the next two, maybe three weeks? Nothing else besides that? And after, I'm free of this God-forsaken town and its stupid traditions."

"That's correct, Ms. Reed."

"Do I have to attend any of the festivities?"

"Your father did not stipulate that in his will."

Harper breathed a sigh of relief. "So I can lock myself away in the house for the next few weeks? I don't have to interact with anyone? I don't have to go anywhere or participate in anything until it's time for the estate sale?"

"That is my understanding," Wilton answered. "But, Ms. Reed, as a friend of your father's, I would ask you to at least try. The Cookie Throwdown starts in a few hours. You know it's always a fun event. Or the candlelight ceremony is in just a few days on Christmas Eve. This year, we're even doing a Christmas rock concert at the amphitheater. I believe they're calling it Merry Rock-Mas.

"You might run into some of your old friends," he continued hopefully.

"No, thank you. That, more than anything else, would be a reason to lock myself away and not come out."

"Oh, Harper," Wilton said in a patronizing tone. He rearranged the papers on his desk, tucked the will back into its manila folder, and leaned back in the chair. The excruciating scream resonated one last time. "I remember you had quite the crush on..."

"Nope," she interrupted. "Don't say it. This isn't one of his damn Christmas movies. Please, hand me the keys and file the paperwork so I can be done with all of this."

With keys in hand, she stormed out of Wilton Johnson's office.

Harper held the wine glass in her hand. A light layer of red clung to the inside of the glass; the last remnants of the Merlot she'd just finished off. Soft Italian music played over the speakers.

She glanced in the mirror that hung over the bar across from her. Harper wanted (no, needed) a glass or three of wine. Luigi's had always served the best wine in town, so once she left the attorney's office, she headed straight there. She wasn't hungry, opting to head straight to the bar and sit on one of the cushioned barstools instead.

While eyeing herself in the mirror, she also noticed she was the only one at the bar.

"Slow afternoon?" she asked the bartender as she tapped on the brim of her empty glass.

He popped the cork on another bottle and poured. "Cookie Throwdown is going on. Most of the town's there." He raised the bottle, put a stopper in it, and set it aside. "You look familiar," he continued. "Do I know you?"

"Nope, just one of those faces," she lied.

"Well, you should stick around. This town really lights up during the holidays, especially on Christmas Eve."

"So I've been told." She fought the urge to roll her eyes.

Harper watched herself take a long sip of the freshly poured red. Behind her, discussion throughout the rest of the small Italian restaurant was muted. Most of the tables were empty. Wine glasses and silverware sat on the unoccupied tables.

No place is more special than Hallmark, except for Disney World.

She heard her father's words echo in her head. He used to say that phrase over and over again. He had said it so much when she was a kid, she had actually believed it. As an adult, though, she knew no place was special, not even Disney World. There was no such thing as real magic. Not even at Christmas time in Hallmark, despite what the movies wanted people to believe.

From behind her, the front door of Luigi's opened. She focused on her glass, taking another delightful sip and pondering if she could truly drink her way from now until the estate sale.

"Table for two, please," a man said.

Fuck.

Harper knew that voice. Knew it too well. It was the only voice that had ever made her hope or wish things could be different. It was the only voice that even now made her wish magic was real. Outside of her father's voice, it was the only other one she couldn't get out of her head. Maybe it was dating all throughout high school. Maybe it was hormonal conditions.

She turned her back and dropped her head, hoping to conceal away anything that resembled herself.

"Harper? Harper Reed?"

Double fuck.

She slowly picked her head up, took a deep breath and released it in a sigh as she did, and spun on the barstool. It'd been just shy of ten years since she'd laid eyes on Brandon Harris.

"Brandon," she said, feigning joy. "It's good to see you. You haven't changed a bit. Still wearing a flannel shirt and blue jeans, I see." She smiled but knew it was as fake as it felt. She hated that it couldn't be genuine. She hated she still, a decade later, felt such strong emotions.

"It's a classic." He returned her smile, but his was genuine. His hand shot to his face, scratching at his brown beard. Harper wondered if he was trying to go for the scruffy lumberjack look or if he'd just stumbled into it.

"Hey, I'm sorry to hear about your dad," he continued. "He'd come down to the station, and we'd chat about, well, just about everything."

"Down at the... you joined the volunteer fire department? Guess it figures. You make the third generation..."

"Fourth," he corrected.

"Fourth generation of Harris's on the Hallmark VFD," she finished. "Congratulations."

"My way of giving back. How's big city life? Your dad kept me up to date on how you were doing...well, as much as he knew of it, at least. He said you two didn't talk often."

"It's good. Love my job, my apartment. Anxious to get back as soon as possible."

"I heard his place is going up for sale. You sticking around while they get everything ready?"

The reminder of her forced confinement to the festive town of Hallmark caused her to reach for the glass again.

"Unfortunately, yes? Pretty much court ordered. Terms of the will, it seems. I have to stay through Christmas, until the estate is sold."

Brandon's smile widened. "Well, that's not so bad. You know how wonderful this place is during the holidays. As your father always said, 'No place is more special than Hallmark, except for Disney World.'" He laughed.

"That he did," she said. "That. He. Did."

"Daddy," a girl's voice piped up from behind Brandon. "Who's the pretty lady?"

Harper had been trying so hard to hide from Brandon that she didn't even notice the little girl in a pretty red dress standing behind him. Harper's mouth fell open. The little girl had called him daddy. Brandon Harris had a daughter! What the hell!

"Well snowflake, this is an old friend of Daddy's. Her name's Harper."

The little girl had red pigtails that draped over her shoulders and onto the red dress. She stared up at Harper with deep green eyes.

"Hi, Ms. Harper. I'm Violet." She extended her hand up to Harper.

Harper grasped it and gave it a shake. "Nice to meet you, Violet."

Brandon bent down next to Violet. "Snowflake, that lady has our table. I'll be right there, okay?"

Violet nodded and skipped over to the table.

Immediately, Harper's eyes shot back over to Brandon. "You have a daughter?"

"Yes, we figured this place would be empty with the Cookie Throwdown going on. I've owed her a nice daddy daughter date for a while. With the holiday season, I've been so busy with the hardware store, I haven't had a chance."

"A daughter," Harper said again. "Brandon Harris, a dad. Part of me never would've guessed it, but then again, Hallmark's special. So, is your wife at the Throwdown, then?"

She didn't know why she'd asked. Harper kept telling herself she didn't care.

You're only here until the sale, remember?

Yes, she remembered, but Brandon was also her first love. Those were the hardest to get over. Him being married helped make it easier.

"Oh, no." His face turned down, and he glanced at Violet sucking down her just delivered Sprite through a straw. "Her mother passed away just over a year ago."

"I'm sorry to hear that."

"It was a tough time. When Summer and I met, Violet was five. After we got married, I legally adopted her. Then, three years into our marriage, Summer got really sick. Doctors said she had a rare bone marrow thing. I think the name of it had every letter in the alphabet. Twice. A year after the diagnosis..."

His voice trailed off.

Harper gently placed her hand on his arm. "Violet's fortunate to have you. She's an angel. You must be doing something right."

"Thanks. Most of the time, she's a demon, but she has her moments." His smile returned. "Speaking of, I should probably go and join her before she ruins her lunch with all the breadsticks. Would you like to join us? Be nice catching up."

As tempted as Harper was, she shook her head. "No, that's okay. I wouldn't want to interrupt your daddy daughter date. Plus, I'm terrible with kids. If we run into each other before I leave, then maybe."

Brandon nodded. "Great to see you, Harper. Take care, and maybe come back again." He strode over to the table and snagged the last breadstick from the basket just before Violet could grab it and inhale it.

Harper and Brandon had had some fun times together, but he was now responsible for a kid. Harper and kids didn't get along. She'd compare it to oil and water, but oil and water mixed better. It was for the best anyway. No reason to spark up an old flame when she also didn't get along with Hallmark.

She turned back to the bar and focused on her wine glass. Glancing in the mirror, she saw Brandon and Violet laughing and smiling.

Good for them.

With another glass emptied, she just sat on her stool, examining the red hue at the bottom of the round glass.

Even though she thought about another glass, she didn't want or need to be here all night.

A loud ring erupted in the dining area, startling Harper out of her wine-induced relaxation. She glanced at the mirror and saw Brandon reaching for his phone. His head nodded as he spoke. When he hung up, he said a few words to Violet who dropped her eyes down to her spaghetti; a sad look on her face. Brandon turned his head to Harper.

Harper tried to avert her eyes, trying not to look as if she'd been watching them.

Brandon stood up and maneuvered over to her.

"I know we haven't seen each other in a while," he said as he got close, "but, Harper, I need a favor."

She bit the inside of her lip and turned on her stool, facing him.

Before she could respond, he continued, "I just got an emergency call. Something happened at the Gingerbread Cookie Throwdown. Not surprisingly, really, but we're shorthanded. Now, I know you said you aren't great with kids, and we haven't seen each other in a number of years, but Violet is great, and she promised to behave for you while I'm gone. Would you mind watching her? It should only take a few hours. If you could take her back to your dad's place, I'll pick her up from there. I've already paid for our dinner. Harper, I'd really owe you. You have no idea."

His pleas flowed out in one single breath, not giving Harper a moment to interject.

She gazed into his eyes and saw the desperation behind them. Once upon a time, she had loved those eyes. That look tugged on her heart strings. She wanted to say no. As she opened her mouth, though, nostalgia wore her down.

"If it'll only be a few hours, that's fine."

"Thank you, Harper. You're the best.

"Snowflake," he hollered. "Come here a second."

Violet scooted back her chair and joined the two of them.

"Snowflake, Ms. Harper is doing us a favor. She's going to take you over to Uncle John's house. Be an angel for her."

Violet smiled up at Harper, and Harper returned the smile. She turned her head to Brandon. "Of course."

Harper unlocked the front door and pushed it open. She hadn't stepped foot in her father's house in almost ten years. Nothing had changed. The smell of his pipe still lingered in the air. The living room furniture hadn't moved. Even the pictures on the wall hung in their same place. The house was a locked time capsule.

As Harper stood just inside the doorway, staring into the living room, Violet rushed past her into the house, nearly knocking her over as she did.

"Hey, there," Harper said. "Be careful. I haven't had a chance to go through anything yet."

"Don't worry. Daddy and I came over to Uncle John's all the time."

Violet ran straight through the living and dining room, slid into the kitchen, and stopped at the refrigerator. She opened it and shuffled items around.

Since it was obvious that Violet had been here before, Harper turned back to the car, remotely popped the trunk, and grabbed her suitcase. She wheeled it up the sidewalk and stepped through the doorway.

"What the hell do you think you're doing?" Harper forcefully asked Violet.

Violet sat on the rocking chair with a Miller Lite in her hand. She took a huge swig and smiled at Harper.

"I know. Miller Lite isn't my favorite either, but it's the only thing he had in the fridge."

"I'm not the best with kids, suck actually, but I doubt Brandon - your dad - would want you drinking beer. How about you hand that to me?"

She left her suitcase next to the door and marched over to Violet.

"If you touch this beer, I'm going to rip your fucking arm off and beat you with it."

Harper had never been physically punched in the stomach, but she imagined this felt similarly. Violet was ten years old, maybe eleven, and had just threatened her, violently.

"That's not very nice to say," Harper said, acting stern with her words.

Violet took another gulp from the bottle, belched, and glared at her. "No fucking shit. I didn't say it to be nice." With another swallow, she finished the beer. "How about you make yourself useful and grab me another one?"

"Not happening. And I'm telling your father the moment he walks through that door," Harper said, trying to remain calm.

Violet threw the bottle down, shattering it across the tiled floor. She took a deep breath, held it for a minute with her hand against her chest, then released it, mimicking a calming routine.

"I'm sorry. I shouldn't have been so short with you. Let me start over." Violet cleared her throat. In a voice straight from the ninth circle of Hell, the child said, "Get me a fucking beer."

High pitched, ten-year-old girl giggles rang throughout the room.

Unable to move, Harper stood in the middle of the living room, dumbfounded. Something wasn't right, and for the first time, Harper was afraid.

"Oh, never mind. I don't need another one anyway." She rocked back and forth in the chair. Shards of glass littered the floor. "What would you like to do?"

"I...I don't know." Harper saw the TV remote, bent down, and grabbed it. Her hands were shaking. She struggled to hit the on button. "Want to watch TV?"

"Sure. I got it."

Violet stared at the TV, and it clicked on. The image on the screen started to rapidly change, so fast it was a blur. Then, it wasn't.

"Oh look. A Hallmark Christmas movie! Want to watch one of those?"

Harper found it hard to breathe. She stared at Violet, unable to blink. Quickly, as if almost a twitch, she shook her head no.

"That's right. Uncle John said you didn't like Christmas movies. He said you didn't find this place special. You know what he always said, right?" Violet nodded her head as she spoke.

Harper nodded along with her.

Suddenly, Violet's voice changed again, but this time, it wasn't demonic. It was much more familiar. It was the voice of her father. "No place is more special than Hallmark, except for Disney World." Harper's father's voice echoed throughout her family home.

"How?" she managed to whisper. Tears streamed down her cheeks.

"Because Uncle John's soul is screaming in Hell." Violet answered with a tone like she just answered two plus two equals four.

Harper's legs wobbled. She leaned forward just enough to fall onto the couch as they gave out. Once there, Harper pulled her knees into her chest, curling into a ball and holding herself tight.

"This isn't real. This isn't real," she repeated.

"I know you plan on leaving as soon as you sell Uncle John's house, but, Ms. Harper, I can't let you."

Violet stood and went over to Harper. She gently ran her fingers through Harper's hair.

"My daddy really likes you. I could see it in his eyes every time we came over here. Every time we hung out with your dad.

"Uncle John missed you a lot. If you leave, my daddy will miss you a lot, too. I don't want daddy to be sad. He took care of me after mommy died. He loves me despite knowing what I am."

Harper felt the fingers on her skull. They were like dry ice brushing against her scalp. Absent of life but full of a hellish blaze.

"Ms. Harper, look at me."

Harper didn't want to. Wasn't going to. The last thing she wanted to do was gaze at the demonic spawn that stood next to her, that rubbed its fingers through Harper's hair. She stared at the floor and shook her head.

Suddenly, Violet grasped Harper's face with her hands, digging her palms into her cheeks. She tried to resist, but Violet turned her head, easily overpowering her.

In the same, chilling, otherworldly voice, Violet demanded, "Look at me."

Harper's eyes opened.

In front of her, where Violet's eyes had been, two deep black orbs burned. Harper felt her mind break, but she knew she was too late to do anything about it.

The front door opened, and Brandon stepped inside.

"Wow, something smells good! What are my two favorite ladies cooking?"

Violet, her red dress covered in spots of white flour, came running from the kitchen up to him. She leapt into his arms and Brandon caught her, spinning her and laughing. "Harper's teaching me to bake cookies."

"Cookies?" Brandon asked, intrigued now "What kind of cookies?"

"Snickerdoodle and chocolate chip," Harper hollered from the kitchen. "Some are shaped like Christmas trees and the others..."

"Are snowmen," Violet said triumphantly.

"That sounds wonderful," Brandon said.

He sat Violet down and sauntered into the kitchen. He went to Harper and kissed her on the cheek. "It looks like you and Violet had a great time together." He glanced at Violet and gave her a wink.

"We sure did," Harper said. "How was the Gingerbread Cookie Throwdown emergency, sweetie?"

Brandon saw her eyes reflected off the oven. Somewhere deep inside of those vacant eyes, Harper fought to regain control of herself, but Brandon knew it would be a losing battle. Violet was a very convincing little girl.

After a brief pause, he finally answered. "It was fine. Only a few casualties, but nothing too bad. Most of the gingerbread men escaped. They'll be popping up all over town, I'm sure."

"That sounds wonderful, dear," Harper said. "After the cookies are done, we can all sit down and watch a Hallmark

Christmas movie. Violet found a good one." She placed her hands on her hips and took a deep, relaxing breath. "You know, my dad used to always say, no place is more special than Hallmark..."

"Except for Disney World," Violet chimed in.

"I don't know," Harper said with a smile. "I think this place gives it a good run for its money.

"Now, who wants cookies?"

CHRISTMAS WITH HIS PARENTS

C andy was bored. She'd said so at least a dozen times. That, along with several other complaints. Complaining was Candy's superpower.

And each time she did, Brett Stephens struggled not to roll his eyes.

"Honey, I'm bored."

"Why are we standing here in the cold?"

"Why did we have to meet your parents over the holidays?"

"You promised me Rockefeller Center."

After the constant barrage, he had finally had enough.

"I thought you might enjoy the Cookie Throwdown. There's only ten minutes left on the clock, but that's fine. We can leave. Take the keys. I'll be right behind you."

"Oh, thank God," Candy Bettencourt said. She grabbed the keys and stomped toward Brett's red Porsche.

Brett turned back to Jason. He and Jason had played football together for Hallmark High. Brett had played quarterback, and Jason had been his favorite receiver. The two hadn't seen each other since Brett left Hallmark for Syracuse. Now that he thought about it, he hadn't seen anyone from high school since he'd moved.

After high school, he'd played football at Syracuse for two years before blowing out his knee. After graduating with his bachelor's degree, he'd met Candy Bettencourt, and his life had taken a new turn.

"Sorry, man. I obviously gotta run," Brett said, pulling himself out of his thoughts.

Jason smiled. "She seems like a delight."

"She has her moments," Brett said, lingering there a few more minutes. "Her parents loaned me the original money to start the dealership."

"How many are you up to now?"

"Currently, four. Another is being built. My face is on more billboards in that one hundred square mile area than I'm proud to admit."

"Her parents loaned you the cash, so you put up with her as a thank you?"

"Something like that. Her parents spoiled her when she was growing up. She definitely knows what she wants when she wants it."

Jason shook his head. "There's only so far a good body gets you. At some point, you have to be a good person. Is she a good person?"

Brett paused. He wouldn't describe Candy as high maintenance. That didn't seem to go far enough. She didn't have a single habit or routine that cost under three digits. Most bordered on four. Anytime Brett brought up the necessity of such things, she went on and on about how special she was. "And don't forget, you wouldn't be able to afford me if it wasn't for the loan," she would remind him.

Before Brett could answer, as if he even needed to, Jason asked, "You guys heading to your parents next?"

Brett nodded his head. He glanced across the crowd and over to the clock above the judges' table. It showed five minutes. Candy had been waiting in the car for almost five minutes. He could only imagine what she'd say when he joined her.

As his eyes dropped away from the clock, he saw a familiar face toward the front of the crowd. His hand started to rise, but Evelyn turned away before it was even halfway up. He awkwardly lowered it. Thankfully, Jason hadn't noticed.

"They haven't met her, have they?" Jason asked, knowingly.

"This is the first time I've been back to Hallmark since I graduated. I've been so busy with the business. I've talked about her to them, but no, they haven't met her."

"You think they're going to like her?"

Brett shook his head. "They're going to hate her."

Jason placed his hand on Brett's shoulder. "Brett, you took us to state with that golden arm of yours. Make sure your gold digger girlfriend doesn't steal it off you."

"You're an asshole, but I love you." Brett hugged Jason. "Enjoy the Throwdown. Cage is all set and ready." He pointed at the car. "I'm going to go face the wrath."

Brett jogged to the car and saw Candy sitting in the passenger seat, examining herself in the mirror, and reapplying her lipstick.

"What took you so long?" she whined. Brett tried to hide a wince. Her nasally voice could wake the dead.

"Saying goodbye. With friends you haven't seen in a while, it can take some time."

"Why would you be friends with people here?"

"I grew up here," Brett said, starting the car.

"I know, sweetie. And yet, I love you anyway." She patted his cheek, patronizingly. "I thought when Daddy bought you the dealership, you had put all of this behind you."

Brett took a deep breath. "We're just staying for the day," he said slowly and controlled. "Plus, I haven't seen my parents in a few years. They want to meet you. I'm sure my mother has made a huge dinner for us." He saw the look on her face. "We can leave right after dinner."

She let out a loud sigh. "I guess I can survive in this little backwoods Christmas town for a few hours."

"At night, it's really pretty. The streets are lit with Christmas lights. Usually, it's snowing. It's better than Rockefeller Center."

Candy clutched her stomach and laughed. Midway through, she snorted. "Oh, Brett. You are so funny." She stopped laughing, and her face became dead serious. "There's nothing better than the City. Do you have a Michael Kors or a Saks here? I don't think so." She tucked her lipstick back in her purse. "Come on. Let's get this over with."

Harold and Julie Stephens rushed out of the house as Brett swung the car into the driveway. Harold wore gray sweatpants, a matching sweatshirt, and house slippers. Julie wore a white skirt and a red Christmas shirt. A white apron with Santa on the front hung around her neck.

Brett opened his door and stepped out of the Porsche.

"Mom! Dad!" he hollered.

Julie ran up to him and gave him a hug and a kiss on the cheek. Harold gripped his son's hand and gave it a good shake, while Julie still wrapped her arms around his stomach.

"Oh, we've missed you," Julie said, excited.

Harold glanced into the car. "Is she staying in the car all evening?"

Brett broke free of his mother's hug and hopped to the passenger side of the car. He opened the door and extended his hand.

Candy grabbed it, easily rising out of the car. She adjusted her tight leggings and strolled over to Harold and Julie.

"You must be Candy," Julie said. She held out her hand.

Candy shook it with only a few fingers as if she'd catch something by touching too much of it.

"I am. It's nice to be here." Candy glanced at the front of the house. "It looks so very...quaint."

Brett lowered the passenger seat and grabbed a few presents stashed behind it.

"Brett, you shouldn't have," his mother said.

"I couldn't come empty handed," he responded, closing the door and heading up the driveway just behind the other three.

"Set those under the tree. I'm almost done cooking Christmas dinner."

"Mom, you didn't need to go all out for us."

"Nonsense," Harold responded. "It's been so long since we've seen you, your mother figured she owed you a good hearty meal. Plus, she's cooking up everything today since you won't be here on Christmas. Even made gingerbread men, but don't worry. Her cookies obviously aren't competing."

As they stepped into the house, the aroma hit Brett. The smells took him back to his youth, to Christmases as a kid, excitedly opening one present on Christmas Eve, before rushing off to bed, anxious to find out what Santa would bring the next morning.

He missed the simplicity of life in Hallmark.

"Candy, do you enjoy cooking? You can help me in the kitchen."

Candy turned her nose up, and a confused look shot across her face. "Cooking? Oh no. These hands don't go anywhere near food."

"Oh, okay then," Julie said. "Well, come join me in the kitchen at least. I'd love to get to know you while Brett and Harold catch up."

Julie slid her arm around Carol's waist and led her away.

"That's an interesting lady, you found yourself," Harold said as he sat down in his rocking chair.

The Christmas tree sat in the corner. Brett could've crawled to it blindfolded. That had been its place his entire life. He knew the lot his dad had bought the tree from, the kind of tree, and probably could've guessed what row the tree had been on. Nothing ever changed in Hallmark, and although he used to long for more, now that he was back, he found himself missing those things that stayed constant. Like a good Christmas in Hallmark.

He sat the presents down under the tree, then strode past his dad and over to a hutch against the wall. The top of it had pictures of him from high school and college. He saw one with him one knee in his varsity football uniform. The same picture every player had to take. Another was an action shot someone had taken of him getting hit just as he threw the football. His hand hovered next to one of him and Evelyn. She was under his arm, gazing up at him with lovestruck eyes.

"Still surprised you two broke up," his dad said from his recliner.

"Different goals."

"She wanted to stay here, and you had your scholarship. If you would've asked, she would've gone with you."

"All in the past. I'm with Candy. Her parents loaned me the money for the dealership." Brett kept his eyes on the picture of him and Evelyn.

"And that makes it alright for you to not be happy?"

Brett turned away from the picture and headed back to the couch. "Candy's great...once you get to know her."

"How much does she contribute versus how much does she cost?"

"Dad, I do pretty well."

"That's what I mean. Brett, I know you do well. But there are girls out there who will only be with you because you do well. It's all about the latest gift you can buy them. The latest trip you can take them on. If the dealership was struggling, if you didn't have a Porsche in my driveway, would she still be interested?"

"Candy grew up expecting a particular standard of living."

"I'm not against a particular standard of living. Your mom and I don't struggle, but we also understand there are more fulfilling things in life. Growing up in Hallmark should've taught you that. Christmas isn't about the material things you get, but the joy you give others. Does Candy know that? Does she experience joy in giving or only in getting?"

His dad was right. Brett knew Candy was a gold digger. If the car dealership ever started to have problems, she wouldn't stick with him. She'd be gone, seeking the next guy who her parents put their money behind. The next guy who would keep giving her things.

He needed to find happiness again. His eyes drifted back to the hutch top. Although he couldn't physically see the picture of Ev, he knew it well enough to visualize it.

"You're right, Dad," Brett admitted. "You're absolutely right." He sighed. "I need to break up with her. I'm not happy. Their daughter shouldn't be a stipulation of the loan."

"I'm glad you feel that way. Your happiness is important to us."

"Boys," Julie called from the kitchen. "Who's ready for dinner?"

"It smells great, and I'm starving," Harold said loudly. He stood up from his chair and marched to the dining room. "By the way, your mother and I have a gift for you."

Brett stood up and followed him, protesting. "You guys didn't have to get me anything."

The table looked just as it should for a Hallmark Christmas dinner. Four place settings were equally spaced along the round table. A large Christmas turkey, much too large for the four of them, sat in the center. Stuffing, mashed potatoes, gravy, cranberry sauce, and vegetables surrounded it.

As Brett passed Candy, she turned and rolled her eyes. "I told your mother that I'm a strict vegan, and that you're on a very strict diet. I don't believe there's a single thing here we will be able to eat. Everything has something made from an animal with a side of fat."

Brett sat down to her right and Harold sat on her left, closest to the turkey. Julie hadn't come out of the kitchen yet.

"What about the vegetables?" Brett asked.

Candy took a frustrated breath. "She put butter in them. Butter. It's as if they don't want us to eat. We should go. We should just leave. Right. Now. This is insulting. That's what it is."

Brett glanced over at his dad. Behind his dad's eyes, a whole conversation played out between the two of them.

"Julie, are you ready?" Harold asked.

"Coming out now," she answered, appearing with a large sheet of plastic.

Harold stood up. "It's nice to celebrate the holidays together. Christmas is a time of giving." He slid the turkey closer and grabbed the carving fork and knife. "This, Brett, is our gift to you."

Julie tossed the plastic sheet over the table, covering the food and place settings.

The moment it settled onto the table, Harold took the carving fork and shoved it into Candy's temple. Her mouth dropped open in a silent scream, and her eyes bugged out of her head. He used the buried fork to pull her head closer, and then dragged the carving knife across her throat. A stream of dark red blood spewed from her carotid artery, showering the plastic sheet.

Candy's body twitched for a few moments as her heart pumped its remaining blood down the front of her sweater.

Harold, still holding onto the fork, leaned her head back, spreading open the cut that ran across her throat. He placed the sharp knife into the fatal wound and sliced back and forth, carving deeper and deeper into her neck until it fell completely backward. Only the spinal cord held it in place.

"Dear, let me help," Julie said.

She moved around the table holding a pair of kitchen shears. When she reached Candy, she opened the sheers and cut through the remaining bone and tendons. If not for Harold holding the carving fork still buried in her temple, it would've rolled onto the floor. Instead he held it up.

"Son, our gift to you."

Brett stared at the head of his girlfriend. Her headless corpse lay slumped in the chair next to him.

"I...I don't know what to say," Brett said. He took a deep breath and smiled. "Thank you so much. This means the world to me." Tears filled his eyes. "This is probably the greatest gift you've ever given me."

Julie and Harold smiled from ear to ear.

"We've never been happier," Julie said, her own eyes tearing up.

"What do we do now?" Brett asked.

Julie rolled up the bloodied plastic sheet. "I'm going to dispose of this. Harold, take Candy out back for the dogs to enjoy. She doesn't have much meat on her bones, so it won't take them long. Brett, you eat up. I didn't make all this wonderful food so it can go to waste. And after dinner, maybe give Evelyn a call. I hear she's still sweet on you."

A Prince in Hallmark

With only a few days until Christmas, Jonathan Fields drove as fast as he could down the small highway which led into Hallmark.

"Are you sure this is where you'd like to spend the holidays, sir?" he asked.

From the backseat of the Audi A8, the Prince raised his head, gazing at his driver. He'd been lost in thought as they drove through the scenic trees and countryside. The landscape reminded him of the woods he had played in as a child. He used to spend hours running the rolling green hills, laughing as his father chased after him.

"In all my travels and of all the pictures I've seen," the prince said, "this town, more than any other, reminds me of the movies. For once, I want to spend the holidays in a small town where no one knows who I am. I can walk the streets without a mob of people. I can dine quietly without hassle. I can visit a bar and have a normal conversation."

"And meet a normal girl who might fall in love with you for who you are and not your title?" Jonathan finished.

The Prince smiled. "This place reminds me of the movies, Mr. Fields. I didn't say I wanted to reenact one."

"True, but, sir, look at yourself. You have your boyish good looks, your perfectly styled black hair, your excellent sense of style, and your hint of a British accent. If this was a movie, you'd fit the mold of the dapper young gentleman to a tee."

The Prince glanced down at his Armani suit pants and white silk shirt. The matching suit jacket gently lay on top of the monogrammed garment bag which sat across the matching monogrammed luggage. He ran his fingers through his short black hair and smiled, knowing how right his personal valet was. If this was a movie, he'd have the lead role.

As he thought about it, though, he realized that wasn't his goal. He wanted to be invisible, be a normal person visiting a normal small town. Currently, he appeared like a prince. He needed a new look to not draw attention to himself.

"How much further until we reach Hallmark?" he asked.

"We have another hour before we reach the cottage. Is everything alright, sir?"

"No, Jonathan, everything's not alright."

A worried look shot across Jonathan's face. "What do you need, Your Highness?"

"New clothes."

"New clothes?" The look on Jonathan's face went from worried to confused.

"If I want to be invisible, blend in as they say, I can't very well do it in a custom Armani suit. I must look the part. My appearance practically screams royalty. The paparazzi will be on me in no time. I'd like to spend the few days left until Christmas in peace."

"New clothes," Jonathan said, nodding his head in understanding. "Your Grace, do you have a place in mind to find these new clothes?"

"Find a town between here and Hallmark. Any store will do. Find me a few pair of blue jeans, a few Christmas sweaters, and maybe even a hat." The Prince placed his hand to his face, thinking. "Oh, and Jonathan, while we are in Hallmark, you must stop with the 'Your Grace', 'Sir', or 'Your Highness'. That will give the game away."

"What would you like me to call you?"

"How about...Gary?" The Prince asked.

"Gary?" Jonathan asked. "Why Gary?"

"I don't know. I've always liked the name. It's very plain. I believe it suits me."

"Gary it is, then, your...Gary." Jonathan stuttered, struggling not to address the prince as he usually would. "What about your last name?"

"Lee," the Prince said. "While we are in Hallmark for the holidays, my name is Gary Lee. Oh, and I'll be driving myself around as well."

"Yes, sir, Mr. Lee."

"Jonathan, just call me Gary."

"It'll be difficult, but I'll try...Gary. It looks like there's a small town ahead just before we reach Hallmark. I'll purchase new attire."

"Thank you, Jonathan. That'll be great."

Gary eased back against the seat and stared out the window. Tall trees zipped past on both sides of them. Light patches of white snow clung to their branches.

With a smile on his face, he eagerly anticipated his next week in Hallmark. Christmas was four days away. He'd heard such wonderful things about the small, picturesque town. A vacation from his normal routine, from the mobs of people, would be a welcome relief. And if he did happen to meet someone interested in him and not because of his title, well, stranger things had happened.

As the sun fell below the horizon, the town of Hallmark truly began to shine. Christmas lights lit the sidewalks. Handrails glowed with strands of garland. Wired decorations strung with multicolored lights blazed to life in the city park. Some decorations had lights that turned on and off, giving an illusion of movement. A light display of Santa tossing presents into his sack. Another had a few reindeer playing instruments. With the addition of the brisk northern breeze and the light snowfall, nothing could be more beautiful, or perfectly capture that image of Christmas, than downtown Hallmark.

Gary, dressed in his blue jeans, an ugly Christmas sweater with a drunken goat in a Santa hat on the front, and a wool hat with flaps covering his ears, quietly strolled the downtown walkway. He passed the courthouse and its large Christmas tree in front. A flyer in his cottage had advertised a candlelight ceremony in front of this very tree in just two nights. He had added it to his calendar to attend. He planned on doing all the normal holiday things that normal people do during their normal holidays.

While he ventured through town, others did as well. They stared directly at his face, at his eyes, smiled, and wished him a merry Christmas. No one gave any indication that they recognized him. He was invisible. A nobody. Another random visitor to this quiet town. He was free to roam the streets without a mob of people.

He smelled the sweet aroma of candy and paused in front of a confectionery. The store had a large window in front, allowing him to peer all the way through the shop. The smell beckoned to him, but he wasn't quite hungry yet. Instead, he continued admiring the large Christmas

Ferris wheel decorated in the window. Little gingerbread men rode on the Ferris wheel. As Gary watched them go round and round, one of them turned to him and waved. He smiled and waved back. Such an interesting little candy shop with gingerbread men decorated as soldiers, chefs, and smiths.

The Hallmark Public Library sat at the end of the street. He knew no one would be there at this time of night. Even though it was closed, it was still festive. Multicolored Christmas trees shone in the windows, casting an assorted array of colors on the sidewalk.

Gary Lee turned and slowly strolled back up Main Street. With the moon waxing in the night sky, he took a deep breath of the cold, fresh air and exhaled.

After passing more shops and boutique stores, a few eateries, and a hardware store, he wandered his way back to the Audi. He'd driven himself into town, although Jonathan had asked Gary multiple times if Gary wanted him to drive.

"It really isn't necessary," Gary had told him. "I've managed on my own before."

Reluctantly, Jonathan had let his prince explore Hallmark on his own, and Gary couldn't have been happier for the solitude. Jonathan meant well. His family had worked for Gary's for many years. Gary often treated Jonathan as part of the family. And although Gary usually enjoyed Jonathan's company, there were times he wanted to be alone.

He knew Hallmark would be quiet enough to allow him that freedom, and he wasn't disappointed.

Gary clicked the button to unlock the car, and the chirp echoed out. As the head and taillights flashed, something seemed off. Gary clicked the button again, and the lights flashed once more. The angle of the car was off - tilted. He leaned his head as he approached the Audi and realized what was wrong. The driver's side back tire was flat. It wasn't just low; it was completely flat. The rim squished the rubber under the car's weight.

"Oh, lovely," he said to the night sky.

His first instinct was to call Jonathan to change it, but then he stopped. He knew how to change a tire. He wasn't helpless. It might've been a while, but he was confident he could do it. Royalty didn't make him helpless. Quite the opposite.

With a click of the key fob, the trunk swung open. Gary lifted the covering and found the spare tire and jack. He removed both and sat them next to the car. He glanced at the dirt and gravel on the ground, along with the darkened patches of snow, and realized it was time to get his hands and jeans dirty.

After loosening each lug nut, he knelt on the ground next to the car and slid the jack underneath. With both hands on the ground, he lowered his body all the way to the cold asphalt and sat the jack in the right place. Within a few minutes, he had the car up and the flat tire removed. He grabbed the spare, slid it on, and used his fingers to tighten each lug nut. He'd use the tire iron once the car wasn't on top of the jack.

Gary stood back for a minute from the car, admiring his handy work. He glanced at his filthy hands and smiled. Been a few years since he'd had to get himself dirty. He quite enjoyed it.

Headlights pulled in behind him, illuminating the entire parking area as if it was daylight. The door swung open, and a female voice cried out.

"Need a hand?"

He turned his head and squinted against the brightness. There were two harsh lights from the front of the large truck as well as a row of lights on top.

A beautiful, black-haired woman hopped out of the truck and stood at the edge of the parking lot. She was dressed in overalls. The truck lights behind her silhouetted most of her features, making her little more than a shadow.

"No, thank you. I'm just about to lower it," he said, trying to hide his accent as best he could.

Since he now had an audience, it was time to finish the task. He stepped back to the car, bent down to the jack, and released it.

The car slowly fell to the ground. The tire touched down, and the car kept going. The rim once again embedded into the rubber.

"Looks like your spare is flat," the black-haired lady said. "Are you sure you don't need a hand?"

Defeated, and trying his best to hold back his anger, Gary threw his hands behind his head and stepped away. He was so furious, he could kill someone. After pacing and taking a few deep breaths, he regained his composure.

"It seems that I may actually need your assistance," he finally said.

"It's not a problem." She strode over to him. "My name's Yvonne. Yvonne Wolfe with an E. Owner of Moonlight Towing." She held her hand out, and he shook it.

"Lee. Gary Lee. How did you happen to know I needed assistance, Mrs. Wolfe with an E?"

"I drove past and noticed you had a flat. I assumed anyone driving an expensive car might not want to get themselves dirty. By the time I spun around, you were almost done. I was twice surprised. You didn't mind getting dirty and you changed that tire pretty quickly."

"Yes, but unfortunately the spare..." he said, trailing off. He realized he hadn't been hiding his accent very well, and Yvonne had a curious look on her face.

"Not from New England, are you?" she asked.

"No, that I am not." He brushed his hands on his jeans. "Do you happen to have a spare tire on you?"

She laughed and shook her head. Gary was captivated by her emerald eyes and sultry voice. She wore bright red lipstick. There was an alluring quality about her.

"I can air up your spare. Hopefully, it doesn't have a hole in it also. I'll take your tire back to the shop and have it fixed in the morning. Swing by after ten, and I'll swap it out for you."

"That sounds perfect. Thank you, Mrs. Wolfe with an E, for all of your assistance."

She went back to the truck and grabbed a portable air compressor. She carried it to the Audi, set it down, and removed the stem cap from the tire. The compressor roared to life, pumping air into the flattened spare tire.

Gary watched it inflate. He held his breath, hoping the tire would stay true. Once the compressor shut off and the tire maintained the car's weight, he exhaled.

Yvonne grabbed the tire iron and tightened the lug nuts. She picked up the air compressor and flat tire and carried them to her truck, tossing both onto the bed with ease.

She reached into the truck's cab, grabbed something, and marched back. She held her business card out to him.

"Swing by in the morning. Oh, and it's Ms. Wolfe, not Mrs."

He grasped the business card but didn't look down at it. Instead, he held on her emerald gaze. "Pardon me for the error, Ms. Wolfe."

Gary smiled as she drove off with his tire.

Although the prince was much more of a night person and hated waking up early, he made a point to be up and out of the cottage well before ten. All night, every time he closed his eyes, he saw the green glow of Yvonne's. He struggled to remember the last time he'd been so captivated by someone in such a short amount of time. Had he ever?

Ignoring his despise for the early morning sun, he drove the hobbled car to the address on her business card, grateful for the strong window tint. Typically, Jonathan would handle these matters, but he wanted to handle this personally. Gary knew that Jonathan would wake up soon and immediately be worried about where he was. He'd left Jonathan a note, hoping to curtail any panicked calls.

Moonlight Towing was the first business on Main as Gary drove into Hallmark. The large tow truck sat in the front. He swung his car into one of the few parking spots. Through the glassed building front, he saw Yvonne sitting in the small waiting area behind a metal desk, her head down, working on paperwork.

As the car came to a stop, she picked her head up. She slid back from the desk and stood up, placing her hands in the pockets of her overalls and stepping out of the office.

"Good morning, Mr. Lee," she said as he swung the door open. She extended her hand.

"And a good morning to you, as well, Ms. Wolfe." He rose out of the car and shook her hand. "I hope you slept well."

She smiled, her red lipstick stretching across her face, showing off her perfectly straight white teeth. "Haven't made it to bed yet. I do most of my work in the late hours of the night."

"Moonlight Towing. The name is quite fitting then."

"You have no idea."

"Have you had time to examine the tire?" he asked.

"Yes, I did. Unfortunately, the damage was in the sidewall and not repairable. Been a rash of that happening since the gingerbread throwdown. Little gremlins. I don't have a replacement available but can order one. How long do you plan on being in town? I should have it the day after Christmas."

"The day after Christmas? Well, that works out wonderfully actually. I plan to spend the holidays in this lovely little town of yours."

Yvonne used both hands to brush her jet-black hair behind her ears. "I don't know if you've noticed, but you picked the perfect time. Christmas is our thing. Some say it's magical here this time of year."

"I've quite enjoyed the decorations. The people of Hallmark are so very nice, present company included."

Gary saw an attractive hint of red splash across her cheeks.

"Ms. Wolfe..." he started.

"Please, call me Yvonne."

"Of course. Yvonne, I saw a flyer for a candle lighting ceremony at the large Christmas tree tomorrow evening. In such a spirited town as this, are there other celebrations happening?"

"Yes, there is. There will be a Christmas concert tomorrow evening. Of course, with it being Christmas Eve, it will snow. It always snows on Christmas Eve. Part of the magic."

"Snow falling and a Christmas concert. Both sound rather delightful. I'm positively thrilled I will be spending my holidays here."

Gary turned back to his car, but then hesitated. "Yvonne, one last question if, I may." He no longer tried to hide his accent.

"Ask away," she said, following him to his car.

"What would you recommend for a nice dinner? Especially one with good refreshments." He stared into her eyes, drawn in by them.

"There's Luigi's, if you're a fan of Italian."

"I'm a fan of Italian red, but not as much of the food. Too much garlic. Tends not to sit well with me." He paused for a moment, but then continued. "But, if you would allow me the pleasure of your company and would prefer to dine there, I would be most pleased to accompany you while you dine. My treat, of course. Consider it a thank you for helping me with the car last night."

"Mr. Lee, I must warn you. This is a small town. If we're scene in public together for an elegant dinner, it may stir up gossip."

"I don't mind being seen in public with a charming and beautiful woman. If that creates gossip, I'd be flattered by the rumors."

Yvonne laughed. "You aren't the one who lives here. That being said, I couldn't care less about rumors. I'm sure if you ask around, you'll hear plenty about me." She leaned in close to him, and said in a conspiratorial mock whisper, "Only pay attention to the bad stuff."

Now Gary laughed. "You are quite cheeky, Yvonne. Shall I pick you up here at seven."

"That sounds lovely," she said, trying to imitate his accent.

He laughed again, got back in the car, and drove back to the cottage.

"Your Highness, do you think you should be going out on a date?" Jonathan asked.

"Relax. It's not a date. I'm saying thank you for her assistance," the prince responded while combing his hair.

He was dressed in a pair of slacks and a button-down shirt. Both of which Jonathan had to purchase for him just hours earlier.

"Not a date? Sir? Do you seriously believe that? Based on how you've described her, she sounds like your type. Add in the fact that she doesn't know your title...it's starting to sound like one of those Christmas movies."

"Jonathan, you are not quite as funny as you'd like. Yes, she's beautiful. Yes, she's alluring. Yes, there's something about her that's different than others. That doesn't mean I'm going to fall hopelessly in love and want to marry her. We are simply going to dinner."

"At an Italian restaurant," Jonathan stated. "You hate Italian. So, will you be dining with her, or shall I have something prepared for you later in the evening?"

The prince glanced up at Jonathan and rolled his eyes.

"I might snack before I leave."

Yvonne leaned forward onto the table.

Gary talked about what he'd seen of the town so far. The quaintness of it as much enamored him as everyone else who passed through. She didn't mind listening to him, though. There was something captivating about the way he spoke. It left her disarmed.

When most men saw her, their minds immediately thought of one thing. It only took staring into their eyes, seeing where their eyes fell on her body, for her to know. For those men, ripping the heads off their bodies and gnawing on their flesh felt like such irony. They'd love to sink their teeth into her, so instead, she would sink hers into them.

But Gary Lee felt different. She found herself unusually intrigued. Part of her wanted to escort him out to the lake and dance in his blood, the beast part of her, but the other part of her...well, those thoughts led to her blushing like a schoolgirl.

She gripped her knife and fork and sliced into the rare steak on her plate.

"When you said this was an Italian restaurant," Gary said, pointing to the slab of meat, "I didn't quite expect that."

"Luigi's is the best Italian food in Hallmark, but they also have the best steaks. The chef is a personal friend. He knows just the way I like it."

Yvonne scarfed down the piece of steak. Red liquid dripped off her fork and spread across her plate.

"By just the way you like it, I assume it's one step away from living." He sipped on the red wine. The table was empty in front of him except for his glass.

"Cooked just enough to be healthy, but not enough to burn out the flavor," she countered.

"Touche," Gary responded and smiled.

She ate more of her steak, the blood oozing from the barely cooked meat.

"Your accent," she started. "European? Slightly British, but not exactly."

"Ah, yes, the lovely game of an American guessing a nationality based on an accent. I shall be that mystery wrapped in an enigma."

"Everybody's from somewhere, Mr. Lee. By the way, at some point I'd love to learn your real name. I doubt it's Gary Lee. You don't look like a Gary Lee."

"I've traveled extensively. Grew up in one place. Schooled in another. Where I'm from is a difficult question to answer. You could say I'm an amalgamation of a lot of places and cultures."

Yvonne watched his eyes as he spoke. They shifted from side to side. He spoke eloquently but answered nothing, dodging questions. Behind his deep gray eyes, he was hiding something. But she couldn't quite put her finger on what it was. Not yet anyhow.

His eyes shifted back to hers and held them. Their gray reminded her of smoke, trapped within a glass. She wanted to look away but couldn't. He entranced her.

The entire feeling unnerved her. She was the aggressor. The alpha of the pack. Yet, she felt like a giddy schoolgirl in love for the first time. That wasn't going to work. She needed to be the dominant figure. Not so easily captured by whatever alluring mystery lay behind his smoke-filled eyes.

"How'd you like to go see another part of Hallmark?" she asked.

Once dinner was finished, she asked to drive his car.

"It's hard to explain where we're going. It's easier if I just drive."

Despite his initial resistance, Yvonne convinced him. She hopped in the driver's seat, and he sat comfortably in the passenger.

"Are you going to tell me where we're going?" Gary asked.

"It's a surprise," she answered.

"As long as you don't plan to drag me out to the middle of the woods and kill me." He gazed at her and smiled.

Oh, you sweet morsel, that'd be a waste.

She laughed. "Oh, please. In this dress?"

"It is quite a stunning dress on you."

She peeled out of the parking lot and drove out of town. The lake was only a few minutes away, especially at night with few people on the roads. The snow fall could get dangerous. Yvonne wasn't worried about that, though.

She just wanted a place to dispose of his car and whatever she didn't eat of his body.

As she pulled up to the edge of the lake, Gary started to chuckle. "You have a bit of a romantic in you, don't you?"

She smiled. "Something like that." She shifted in the seat and glanced over at him. "Tell me the truth. What are you doing in Hallmark? You talked about your travels and education in Europe. You obviously come from money."

"I'd rather not say. I've truly just come here to spend the holidays in a nice, quiet town, far away from anywhere else. That is all. Although I haven't been honest with you about who I am or my real name, please understand it isn't because I hold any ill will toward you. Quite the contrary. I find you intriguing. A rose amongst a field of daisies."

"Holy shit. You're a prince, aren't you?" She flopped her head against the headrest. "Fucking Hallmark. A goddamn prince comes to town, and I end up the maiden. Never in a million years would I have guessed it would happen to me."

"Yes, I am a prince," he admitted. "I implore you not to do anything brash. I only want a nice quiet escape for the holidays."

"I appreciate your honesty, Your Highness. Now, I have a secret for you." Her voice dropped an octave, taking on a guttural tone. "I've never tasted royal flesh before."

Yvonne held her hand in front of her. Her fingers turned into sharp claws and thick, black fur erupted all over her body. Her emerald eyes became laser focused on the fresh meat in the passenger seat. Her nose, mouth, and jaw extended into a snout. Long teeth dripped with saliva, hungry for the taste of royal blood.

To Yvonne's surprise, Gary sat calmly in his chair. If anything, his face showed contempt and anger. How dare he not tremble in fear at the sight of Yvonne the Werewolf, sitting next to him, about to rip his throat apart?

She took a deep breath and released an ear-piercing roar into this face.

Midway through the roar, the prince shot his hand out and gripped her neck with fierce intensity. She'd never felt a grip this strong before. Suddenly, instead of instilling fear in him, she felt terror welling up inside of her. Who the hell was he?

"How dare you?" He spoke very smoothly and deliberately. Anger flashed across his face. Eyes that were once filled with smoke now burned red. He opened his mouth and sharp fangs descended from the roof of his mouth.

"How dare you try to kill me, you petulant mutt?" He shoved her backward, throwing her through the door and into the grassy area. In a flash, he was out of the car and standing on top of her.

She quickly transformed back into her human form. Naked, she tried to scurry away. She'd never been so terrified in her life.

He grabbed her leg and flung her against the side of the car.

Struggling, she asked, "Who are you?"

"I am Prince Vlad Tepes of Wallachia."

He bent down, gripped her black hair, and lifted her off the ground.

"Some have called me Vlad the Impaler. Others have called me the Devil himself. But you," he said, pulling her close to his face, "you can call me Dracula."

She trembled at the name, suspended naked in the air.

With a flick of his wrist, her neck snapped. Although still alive, she lost feeling in her limbs. She had the ability to heal, but a wound such as that would take days to recover, if not weeks.

Still holding her by the hair, he spun in a quick circle and heaved her broken body into the middle of the lake. She crashed through the thin layer of ice and sank to the bottom. As the moonlight disappeared above her, she held her breath as long as she could. She'd never tried to breathe underwater before and wasn't sure what would happen. As her chest burned, she reached the point of no return and took a deep breath of stale lake water.

THE GIRL WHO HATES CHRISTMAS

"Are you sure you don't want to watch a Christmas movie with me?" Lucy asked.

She sat on the couch in Jackie's living room, waiting for her to come out of the kitchen.

Jackie Bessette scoffed loudly enough for Lucy to hear it, despite being a room away. She made a pretend barfing sound.

"Christmas movies are the worst. It's a stupid holiday."

Lucy and Jackie had been dating for six months. This was their first Christmas together. Lucy was excited to be spending it with her girlfriend. She had bought Jackie something special to celebrate. Although Jackie had mentioned her lack of enthusiasm about Christmas, Lucy had laughed it off. They both grew up in Hallmark. It was impossible to not like Christmas, growing up in Hallmark. Cheer and joy spread like a virus within the small town. It was contagious. The Christmas bug had bitten everyone.

Except for Jackie, obviously.

Jackie had avoided answering every time Lucy asked why Jackie didn't like Christmas. Tonight, though, Lucy was determined to get an answer from her.

"I'll put on 'It's a Wonderful Life' and not one of those cliche romantic ones. That's got to be a little better," Lucy pleaded. "It's Christmas Eve. It's not like I'm forcing you to go to the concert or the candlelight ceremony. And hey, didn't you go to the Throwdown? That's Christmas-y."

Jackie came out of the kitchen with a large porcelain bowl of popcorn under her arm. She was dressed in plaid pajamas. "No, the Throwdown was a fight to the death. A miniature WWE." She paused a moment. "Well, it was supposed to be before Goliath ruined everything. And now look. Have you noticed the mayhem around town caused by those little gingerbread shits? Did I tell you one of them jumped on the windshield yesterday? Dive bombed right off a streetlight. He splatted on the car like bird shit, got up, flipped me off, and then jumped onto the road and ran away."

Jackie sat down on the couch next to Lucy and placed the bowl of popcorn in between them.

"Plus, Evelyn was there. You should've seen her face when I pointed out Brett Stephens to her."

"I heard they went out the other night," Lucy said. "The magic of Hallmark. Joy of the Christmas season.

"How about you pick the movie? Scrooged? National Lampoon's Christmas Vacation? A Christmas Carol?"

With each suggestion, Jackie shook her head.

"You're impossible," Lucy said.

"You're really cute when you're angry." Jackie nibbled popcorn off her fingers and smiled.

"It's our first Christmas together. You know I'm madly in love with you. I want to know all your secrets. You've never told me why you hate Christmas. It's just us tonight. I'll turn off the TV. We'll sit here on the couch and share a bowl of popcorn. Spill it. Tell me your story. Tell me the story of the girl who hates Christmas."

"Fine. But, once I tell you, I'm going to have to kill you," Jackie said with a straight face.

Lucy's smile spread. "Ooo. Intriguing. Like you're a secret Russian spy. I'll take my chances."

"Your funeral. It all started when I was eight years old...

It was the day after Thanksgiving – Black Friday. My mother and I were out shopping for a Christmas present for my dad. Everything was on sale. Some stores still do that, but since so much stuff is ordered online now, it's not as fun as it used to be. Since it was so close to Christmas, I figured she had either already bought my Christmas present or had planned to buy me one soon.

As we were shopping, we passed by Toy Emporium. I stopped dead in my tracks. In the window was the Fairytopia Sparkle Barbie. The same one they had made the "Barbie Fairytopia" movie about. She was so beautiful, just staring at me in the window. But then, I raised my head a little higher, and just past the display window, I saw the man himself. Big Red. Santa Claus.

"Mommy, please let me go talk to Santa Claus. Please. There's not a line. There's something I really want for Christmas, and only Santa can get it for me. Please, Mommy?"

My mother had moments where she liked to indulge me. After initially hesitating, she gave in. "Be quick. I'm going to stay right by the door."

"Thank you! I love you!" I said as I ran inside the Toy Emporium.

Only two other kids stood in line in front of me. I bounced in place so much, I probably looked like I needed to pee.

Santa sat on a huge throne surrounded by fake snow. An animatronic Rudolph with his bright red nose bobbed its head up and down as if eating the snow.

A boy hopped onto Santa's lap first. He made wild hand gestures in the air, describing some amazing flying thing he wanted Santa to bring. Santa laughed. After a few moments, the boy jumped down and ran to the back of the store where his mother was.

Next, a little girl, escorted by her mom, stepped up to Santa. He had to lean forward and pick her up so she could sit on his lap. She seemed nervous. Santa had to lean his head in close to hear what she was saying. Eventually, he told her something softly. She nodded and then raised her arms in the air so her mother could pick her up.

It was my turn. I ran up to Santa, bounced off the ground, and landed hard on his lap.

"Wow, you're excited to see Santa, aren't you?" he said in his deep voice, followed by a hardy "Ho Ho Ho" laugh.

"For Christmas, I want a Fairytopia Sparkle Barbie." I spoke so fast, I almost ran out of breath.

"A Fairytopia Sparkle Barbie," Santa repeated.

"Yeah. There's one in the window at the front of the store. I reeeeaaaalllly want it."

"Have you been a good little girl?"

"I've been the best little girl."

"Did you tell your parents you wanted a Fairytopia Sparkle Barbie? I'll check with them before Christmas anyway, but it helps if you've told them."

"Nope. I've just told you," I said with a smile. I was so proud of myself.

"I see. Well, Santa doesn't want to forget and get a different kind of Barbie, so I need you to do me a favor. Santa's getting old. Write it in a letter and mail it to me. Make sure to give the letter to your parents and remind them to put it in the special North Pole mailbag. Can you do that?"

"Yep!"

"Great. Now, run back to your mother and have a Merry Christmas."

I sprinted out of the store and straight into my mom's stomach, giving her a huge hug and a thank you for letting me speak to Santa.

That night, I wrote out my request. I made sure to include the exact type of Barbie I wanted. A Fairytopia Sparkle Barbie. I even mentioned this was to help him out since the elves mess up sometimes. Hopefully, when he read the letter, it'd help him remember me.

With the letter written, I grabbed an envelope, addressed it to Santa via the North Pole, stuffed the letter inside, and licked it sealed. I proudly marched the letter into the living room, but dad was yelling at the football game on TV. Mom was stringing up Christmas decorations. Instead of bothering them, I snuck outside and put the letter in the mailbox. I even raised the flag.

That next morning, the flag was down. I ran outside and the letter was gone! I was so excited. I knew Santa had taken it in the middle of the night.

Come Christmas morning, I tore through the presents my parents had bought me. New clothes, an easy bake oven, and a bracelet making kit. The more presents I opened, the more depressed I became. There was no reason why Santa wouldn't have brought me my Barbie. I had been a good girl all year long.

But then I spied it. Back behind the tree, sat a tall, rectangular box. I reached behind the tree, gripped the package, and slowly slid it out. A card was attached. It read, "Thank you for sending me your letter. I rarely get mail these days. This and many other gifts I give to you, as long as you stay good and do as I say."

Imagine the elation. Not only did Santa bring me the present I wanted, but he was going to give me more gifts.

Lucy listened intently. She sipped on her hot chocolate and occasionally grabbed a handful of popcorn.

"So, Santa said he was going to give you more gifts if you do what he says. Why do you hate Christmas?"

"Stop interrupting. Just listen."

"Sorry. Keep going."

"So, nothing happened for another four years...

Every day after that, I waited for another gift. Of course it didn't happen.

When Christmas rolled around and Santa showed back up in the Toy Emporium, I stormed up to him, furious.

"Why haven't you given me more presents?" I asked... well, demanded.

"Little girl, Santa only makes a delivery once a year...." He started to say in that calmingly deep Santa voice.

"But you said on the card that you'd give me more gifts if I did what you said. You haven't told me anything. That's not my fault."

Santa made a motion with his hand, and the next thing I knew, my father had picked me up. I kept screaming at Santa about him not bringing me more gifts.

My parents tried to ask me what that was all about, but I wouldn't tell them. Christmas came and went. I had a few presents from my parents but nothing from Santa. I didn't understand. I could only assume I was on the naughty list because I hadn't done what he asked. But he hadn't asked me anything! It wasn't fair.

Every day I waited, and every day there was nothing.

Christmas came and went. My parents didn't take me back to see Santa. As you can imagine, I grew to despise that jolly old fuck. By the time I was eleven, if I saw a Santa decoration, I'd sneak out in the middle of the night and destroy it. I can't count the number of Santa blow-ups that I ripped holes into or the number of porcelain Santa figurines that I've smashed.

But then, when I was twelve, almost thirteen, I heard a voice. It came from nowhere but seemed to be everywhere at the same time. It was a few days before Christmas, and I sat at the dinner table with my parents.

"Jacqueline," the voice said.

No one called me Jacqueline. I hated my full name. I always went by Jackie. Even my parents didn't call me Jacqueline.

But someone had.

I glanced at my mom and dad. Both had their heads down, eating my mother's pot roast for dinner.

"Jacqueline," the voice spoke again.

I realized I was the only one hearing anything. All my hatred for Santa faded away instantly. He was speaking to me. My legs bounced uncontrollably. I tried to hide my giddiness.

"I need to go to the restroom," I said. "May I be excused?"

"Yes, go ahead," my dad said.

I left my chair and hurried to the restroom. Once alone, I spoke very softly.

"Yes, Santa?"

"It's time to do a favor for me. I'll give you a gift in exchange."

"Anything, Santa."

"The Santa you spoke to in the past, the one at the toy store, is an imposter Santa. He's poisoning the minds of young children. I need you to kill him."

That made perfect sense to me. Of course that was why he had me hauled away that one year. He wasn't the real Santa. He was an imposter! And for the past few years, he'd been lying to the children of Hallmark. That could not be allowed to continue. I needed to do something about it.

"I'm just a teenager. How do I kill him?"

The voice spoke an idea into my head. It was a sound plan.

Later that night, I snuck into the two locations where Santa had sent me, and then quietly tiptoed my way out of the house. I'd done it plenty of times when destroying Santa decorations, so that part was simple.

As you know, nothing in Hallmark is very far away. I was downtown within twenty minutes. Just as Santa said, the imposter Santa strolled down the street. He still wore his Santa suit. The bastard.

I grabbed the lipstick I had stolen from my mother's sink and put on a heavy glob of it. I also applied a large amount of the eye shadow I had snatched. Once that was done, I sauntered over to the imposter. I had worn an extremely short dress. It had fit when I was ten, but at thirteen, it was way too small.

"Hey, Santa," I said seductively. "How'd you like a little fun with an elf?"

The imposter stopped moving and stared at me. There was hesitation in his glance. Enough that I knew he was interested. Fucking pervert. That was probably why he wanted to be an impostor Santa Claus. He probably touched little kids while they sat in his lap. It was no wonder Santa wanted me to stop him. I was doing Hallmark a favor. Really, the world a favor.

After the hesitation, he continued down the street.

"Oh, come on. I'm sure Mrs. Claus isn't near as pretty as I am."

My steps were faster than his. I gained on him with each passing moment.

"Go away, kid. You're sick," he said, still striding away.

I took a few more steps and was right behind him. I grabbed the box cutters I had taken from the garage and sliced across the middle of his calves. The back of his pants just below his knees fell away and a line of blood flowed down the muscle.

He cried out in pain. As he turned, I was ready. I swung the hammer and connected with his head, just behind his ear. There was a loud crack, and his head spun awkwardly around.

He fell to the ground, gripping his legs with one hand and his head with the other.

I stood over him, holding the hammer. His eyes bulged out of his head, filled with terror. He let go of his legs and raised his hand out in front of him, hoping it would stop me.

But it didn't. Santa had told me what to do, and I wasn't going to disappoint him.

"This will teach you to touch little kids," I said.

The look on his face changed. At the time, I thought it was confusion, but I know it had to be regret. That made much more sense.

I brought the hammer down through his hand and onto the center of his forehead. It bounced back up, leaving a red depression. His eyes rolled back. I swung the hammer again and again, pulverizing his skull. Blood and brain matter rained all over the sidewalk. With each hit, I knew I was saving so many future generations of children from being fondled by this asshole.

When I finally stepped back, there wasn't a head left. Just a pile of flesh mixed with bone shards.

I tossed the hammer, box cutter, lipstick, and eye shadow in a neighbor's trash can on the way back to the house.

Once safely back in my room, I heard the voice. "Excellent job. You've done well. Tomorrow, you shall have an early Christmas present."

I crawled in bed, excited about the next morning. But when I woke up, there was no present. Nothing at all. I had done what he asked. That was our deal. I was supposed to get a gift.

You can't imagine how disappointed I was. I had killed the impostor Santa for him and gotten nothing in return.

Lucy stared at Jackie with a puzzled expression on her face.

"I remember hearing about that murder. They caught the guy who did it. The Toy Emporium Santa was sleeping with the guy's wife or something."

Jackie nodded her head. "That story was a lot more believable than a twelve-year-old with a hammer."

Lucy shook her head. "When I asked why you hated Christmas, I'd hoped you'd be honest with me. Instead, you give me a made-up story of Santa telling you to kill the guy from the toy store."

Frustrated, Jackie said, "I'm not lying to you. I did kill him. And it was because Santa told me to. Or at least, that's what I thought."

"Jackie, are you okay? You look flushed."

"No, I'm not okay." Jackie pressed her hand against her head and shook it back and forth.

Lucy had never seen Jackie this worked up.

"Babe, if we need to pick this conversation up on another day, we can. The last thing I want to do was upset you on Christmas Eve. We can find something to watch and just snuggle on the couch."

Lucy moved the porcelain popcorn bowl from its spot on the couch to the coffee table. She held her arms out, hoping Jackie would crawl across the middle seat and relax against her.

"I can't stop. Now that I've started, I have to finish this."

"Okay...?"

"There's one more confession I have to make."

"Jackie, you know I love you. I've never been happier than with you. You can tell me anything. Whatever it is, we'll get through this together."

"This...this was how I learned the truth...

Three years went by. I never received a gift like I had been told I would. I saved all those kids who could've been abused. Sure, I had to do something bad, which should've landed me on the naughty list. But shouldn't the amount of good outweigh the bad? I thought that would've put me back on the nice list, especially since Santa had told me to do it. Didn't that exclude me from the naughty list?

Day after day. Nothing. No gifts. No voice. Just silent abandonment.

It wasn't long after I turned fifteen that I realized I wanted to be on the cheer squad. I was a freshman at Hallmark High. Of course, to be on the cheer team meant I had to audition. I had the ability to make the team. Had been in tumble classes since I was five. I knew how to do all the stunts. I pretty much had all the cheer routines memorized at this point.

During tryouts, I nailed everything. By the look on the other girls' faces, they were jealous of my ability. I had hit everything perfectly. Probably too perfect. A ballot was passed around to vote on who would be the new additions to the team. I didn't realize it was going to come down to a popularity competition, but that's what happened.

When the tally came in, I was an alternate. Unless something happened to one of the squad, I wouldn't be cheering. I was so upset, I ran into one of the bathroom stalls and cried. It was there, surrounded by those disgusting gray walls, with nothing more than the echoes of my sobs, that I heard his voice again.

"Jacqueline," Santa said. "I have something I need you to do."

"Why?" I cried. "Why should I? I did something for you before and got nothing in return. You lied to me."

"All good things come in time," Santa said. "Just because you haven't received a gift yet, doesn't mean you won't. Santa's a very busy person. But don't despair. This favor will benefit both of us, and I'll be sure to give you extra presents this Christmas."

My crying eased. Extra presents sounded great, so I listened.

A few days passed before it was time to do what he'd asked. Cheer practice had just ended. I watched from the bleachers. The coach wanted me to know the routines, just in case. But for now, there wasn't a reason for me to be in uniform. I sat there, waiting.

Once practice was done, I snuck away. Patiently, I hid.

All the girls funneled into the locker room. They changed out of their cheer uniforms and back into their street clothes. Every few minutes another one or two finished getting dressed and left. The numbers slowly dwindled. The talking and laughing quieted as fewer and fewer were left to participate. I didn't pay attention to what they were talking or laughing about. I stayed focused on what I needed to do.

"Bye, Natalie," Rebecca shouted as she left the locker room. "See you in class tomorrow."

"Later, Becca," Natalie hollered back. She was the only one left in the room. Well, the only one as far as she knew.

I saw her applying the last of her lipstick in front of the mirror. Deadly silent, I slipped over to the light switch and flicked it off. With no windows, the entire locker room plummeted into darkness.

"Hey!" Natalie screamed. "Who turned out the lights? I'm still in here."

I heard her fumbling with her purse, probably searching for her cell.

"Is anyone there? Hello?" Her voice wavered. Fear was setting in.

I crept closer to her. My breath caught in my throat. As far as Natalie knew, not a creature was stirring, not even a mouse. I heard her moving, her breathing, her heart beat with panic. I stood directly behind her in the pitch-black locker room with the tire iron in my hand. I reared my arm back well above my head, then forcefully brought it down in a wide arc.

The metal instrument connected with her knee. A perfect hit. An audible crack echoed in the silent locker room. Silent, just before she screamed in agony. I had enough time to bring it back up and swing down again, connecting in almost the same spot before she crumbled to the ground. When the tire iron hit her leg the second time, there was barely a knee left to stop it. I felt the flesh give underneath, like hitting a sheet blowing in the wind. No hard bone or joint there to stop it.

Natalie cried out. There was such pain in her screams. I'd be lying if I said it didn't make me smile. I had no idea what special naughty list she was on, but who was I to question? Santa knew all. He sees you when you're sleeping. He knows when you're awake. He'd know if you'd been bad or good, and obviously Natalie had been very bad.

Quickly, I hurried out of the locker room. I ditched the tire iron, took a moment to compose myself while listening to Natalie's screams echo, and then ran back to the locker room. I clicked the light on, splashed a worried look across my face, and slid across the floor to her.

"Oh my God, Natalie, what happened?" I asked.

With the light on, I saw my handiwork. The bottom part of her leg stuck out to the side as if knees weren't a thing. Pieces of her leg bone broke through the skin.

Natalie couldn't answer. She just screamed.

I grabbed her cellphone and called 9-1-1.

A few minutes later, the ambulance arrived and took her to the hospital.

Lucy stared at her girlfriend in disbelief.

"I was promoted to the cheer team, and the rest was history."

Lucy had heard the story of what had happened to Natalie. Everyone had. But the story was not that a tire iron had destroyed the girl's leg. The story Lucy had heard was there was a slick spot n the locker room. Natalie had been in a hurry to leave and had slipped. She had fallen so hard onto the unforgiving tile that it shattered her knee cap. The rest of the damage had happened when she had tried to stand and instead fell back down again. She had heard the part about Jackie calling 9-1-1. Jackie was a local hero in Hallmark because of it. In fact, the entire town was grateful. Not only had Jackie saved Natalie from worse injuries, but she had also saved the town's cheer team.

"Santa Claus told you to maim Natalie Tyson," Lucy said. She meant it as a question, but it came out as an accusation.

"That's what I thought," Jackie said.

"And what gifts did Santa give you for doing that, aside from the obvious?" Lucy spoke very slow, still processing what she had just heard.

"The obvious?" Jackie asked.

"Aside from her spot on the cheer team!" Lucy shouted.

"I don't really see that as a present. I put in the work, the dedication. This just made a wrong into a right." Jackie took a deep breath. "But to answer your question. Nothing. Twice Santa told me to do something. Twice I did it, and twice I didn't receive a damn thing. Not then. Not at Christmas. Never. Outside of the Fairytopia Sparkle Barbie, Santa never gave me another present."

"Jackie. Honey. You know Santa isn't real, right? Your parents bought the doll for you that year. And after that, they probably thought you were too old to believe, so they didn't sign any other present from Santa."

Lucy searched for a rational explanation, anything to explain her girlfriend's dissent into madness.

"No. I mean, yeah, that would make sense, but that's not what happened.

"After I did what Santa asked, and he still didn't give me additional presents, my hatred grew stronger. I couldn't stand Santa, really, anything related. Reindeer, elves, all of it. More than once, I thought about moving out of this perfect Christmas town. Santa lied to me again.

"Stop!" Jackie suddenly screamed out.

Lucy flinched backward. She hadn't done anything but listen to Jackie.

Jackie rocked on the couch.

"I knew it was Santa. I knew it to my core.

"After graduation, I moved out of my parents' house. While packing up, I opened a drawer in my desk and found the original note Santa had sent me. The one with the promise he had made. With disdain, I read it again and again. I meant to tear it into a hundred thousand pieces and burn it. But as I gripped it in my hands, I turned it over. I'd never noticed that Santa's note was written on the back of the letter I had originally mailed.

"We're getting to the important part." Jackie shook her head, and then said, "When I'm done, I promise." She hit her temple with the palm of her hand a few times.

"I made a mistake," she continued. "I was eight. I wasn't the best speller. I flipped letters around. I still do it, sometimes. I didn't write my letter to Santa. I wrote it to Satan. He's the one who gave me Fairytopia Sparkle Barbie. He's the one who told me to kill the impostor Santa. And he's the one who told me to take out Natalie."

"Satan?" Lucy asked. "Satan told you to do those things?"

"He's speaking to me now. Again, he's promising me a gift if I do what he says."

"What's he telling you to do, Jackie?"

"Lucy, I love you."

Jackie reached over to the coffee table and grabbed the near-empty bowl of popcorn. She lifted it into the air and slammed it down on the coffee table, shattering it. She grasped a large shard of porcelain in her hand and held it in front of her. Blood poured from her fingers onto the couch as the shard cut into her hand. She stared at Lucy with wild eyes.

"Jackie, I love you, too." Lucy held her hand out in front of her. Tears streamed down her cheeks. "Whatever is wrong, we can fix it. We can get through this."

"I hear him. He promises that this time will be different. He has presents for me. So many presents."

"Please put that down. It's cutting into your hand." Lucy placed a foot on the ground. "Let me get you a band-aid."

"I told you. I warned you. If I told you, I'd have to kill you. That's what I said." Jackie mumbled the words through her own tears. "He wants me to kill you. He wants your blood spilled all over this couch. If I bathe in your blood, all the gifts I have ever wanted are mine."

"Jackie, please. I love you. Let me help you," Lucy pleaded.

"I love you, too. God, I fucking hate Christmas. I'm sorry, Lucy."

Jackie thrust the shard of porcelain into the left side of her own neck and drug it across her throat. Blood spewed from the gaping wound, her carotid artery sending red rivers across the couch and all over Lucy. Jackie gurgled as the blood that didn't squirt from her neck flowed down her esophagus, filling her lungs, drowning her as she exsanguinated.

Lucy screamed as Jackie's dead corpse fell forward.

It was the start of Lucy's hatred of Christmas, as well.

MERRY ROCK-MAS

"Do Re Mi Fa So La Ti Do," Rob Barrett warmed up backstage.

He paced back and forth. Nerves had never been his thing, but for some reason, tonight he couldn't stand still. He glanced in the mirror. Sweat caked his long brown hair against his tanned face. He heard the crowd filtering in. Over the PA system, instrumental Christmas music played.

Christmas. That's what was putting his nerves on edge. It was one thing for him and Sex Leppard to play their usual covers. They just turned all the knobs to max and shredded. He barely had to sing. The crowds knew every song. He'd get them started, and everyone would belt out the lyrics in their usual drunken stupor. Rock 'N' Roll! Fuck yeah!

Why they had agreed to play this one Christmas show, he didn't know. Maybe that was *his* drunken stupor.

Christmas songs were different. Sure, Snow Leppard, the name they had given themselves for this concert, had practiced each song in their own style. It was still going to rock. Some songs were made to crank up. "Carol of the Bells" was about as metal as metal could be. But "I'll be Home for Christmas" had more of that power ballad feel. Power ballads were typically saved for when the crowd was too drunk to care.

Rob stole a glance at the seats as the venue started to fill. There were kids in the audience. He couldn't remember the last time he had played a gig with kids in the audience.

Although Hallmark considered this area "The Amphitheater", it was really nothing more than a covered pavilion with power, bleacher seats, and a lot of open green space at the top.

"You don't look so hot," Eddie Daniels, his lead guitarist, said.

"Just nerves, man."

"Since when do you get nerves?"

"Since we're playing a Christmas concert with kids in the front row. This isn't like playing at a bar. I have to actually sing. Sure, everyone knows the lyrics to 'Don't Stop Believing', but they're usually too drunk to care if I mess them up. If I mess up 'Jingle Bells', well, that's a whole different ballgame."

Eddie clapped him on the back. "Easy enough. Don't fuck up 'Jingle Bells'." He smiled, knowing it wasn't that easy.

"Thanks for the encouraging words. You should go into therapy." Rob shrugged Eddie's hand off his shoulder.

"Where's everyone else?" Rob asked.

"Jason's grabbing the extra snare out of the truck. Scott and Chad are chatting up a few snow bunnies."

"Of course they are", he interrupted. "We've got about thirty until showtime. Gather the band. Make sure everyone's warmed up and instruments are tuned. I'm going to stay here and run some scales."

"Just relax, Rob. The moment you step onto that stage, all the nerves melt away. But don't worry. I'll go help Jason."

Eddie ran off, leaving Rob to continue running scales. It helped his nerves, and after a few minutes, he felt himself ease into his normal rhythm.

A loud crash pulled him out of his reverie.

"Shit! Shit! Shit!" Eddie hollered.

Rob ran past the amplifiers and saw Eddie gripping his hand against his chest. Streaks of blood ran down the guitarist's shirt.

"What the hell happened?" Rob asked.

As he yelled, Jason ran up with paper towels. Eddie pulled his hand away, revealing a large cut down the palm of his left hand. Jason pressed paper towels into the wound.

"I grabbed that metal case; the one with the microphones in it," Eddie said. "A stupid gingerbread man jumped on it. One of the mics started to fall. I tried to catch it. The metal lid snapped down on my hand, and as I pulled my hand out, it cut straight through my fucking palm." His face showed every ounce of pain. "This is bad, man. There's no way I can play tonight."

Rob threw his hands behind his head. "Shit. Fucking gingerbread men! You sure you can't play?"

"I'm going to need fucking stitches, man. It's my left hand. I can't make a single chord right now."

Jason glanced at Rob.

Immediately, Rob knew what Jason was thinking. "No. It's not happening."

"Why not?" Jason asked.

"Because he's a hot-headed asshole, that's why not."

"Dude, it's Christmas. There's a packed house full of people wanting a concert. When was the last time we've played in front of a crowd this size?"

Rob paced again. Jason was right. He didn't want to admit it, but Jason was right.

"He isn't going to know the songs," Rob argued.

"You two played together for so long, he won't have to know them. He knows you. If you said, 'Mary Had a Little Lamb', he'd know what key you were starting in, when you planned to change chords, and when the guitar solo was without asking. You two share one music brain." Jason pressed harder on Eddie's hand. "That's probably the reason you can't stand each other. Too much alike."

Rob grunted forcefully.

"Robert Barrett," Jason said. "Call Randy St. James now."

"Damn it," Rob screamed.

He pulled his phone from his pocket and found Randy's contact. "He's not going to pick up. I guarantee you, he's...Hey Randy, I'm in a little bit of a pickle. It's a long story. Listen, can you get down to the Hallmark Amphitheater? Bring your gear. I'll explain when you get here. I'll owe you."

Rob placed his phone back in his pocket. "He'll be here in five minutes."

For the next five minutes, Jason, Scott, and Chad moved Eddie's rig out of the way and ensured their stuff was handled. Jason's drums, Chad's bass, and Scott's keyboard were in place. All that was left was Randy's gear.

Rob heard the crowd growing louder. Barely an empty seat or blade of grass sat on the lawn. The concert overlapped with the candlelit Christmas tree ceremony, so he knew that not everyone in Hallmark would be there. Some preferred the quieter Christmas Eve. By the look of it, though, a good bit of Hallmark wanted to have their ear drums bleed from a screaming guitar, driving bass, and hair metal style Christmas songs. Fucking rock 'n' roll.

"Does Christmas rock mean you're a sell out?"

Rob shot his head around, whipping himself out of his thoughts.

Randy St. James stood at the back of the stage, his guitar slung around his back, his pedal board in one hand, and his Marshall amp in the other. He'd tied his long blond hair back into a ponytail.

"Have you seen the crowd?" Rob countered. "If you mean sell out by selling out every seat in the house then yes."

"Why'd you call, Rob?" Randy asked. His voice was all seriousness.

"It wasn't my idea. You can sit at home and get wasted on eggnog for all I care." Rob took a deep breath. "It was Jason's idea. We've run into a jam."

"You kick me out of Sex Leppard because I wanted to do a side project, and now you're begging me for my help?" Randy rolled his eyes. He started to turn around.

"First of all," Rob said, "I'm not begging for your help. If you don't want to jam with us, then fuck off. Second, it wasn't because you were doing a damn side project. You started another band. Another 80's hair metal cover band. Why would you think Twisted Roses wouldn't cause an issue?"

Randy sat down his amp and pedal board. He stomped toward Rob, pointing at him. "You wanted Sex Leppard to be all about you. Sure, you're the frontman, but we were a band. You aren't Steve Tyler or Bret Michaels. You're Rob Barret. Your ego pushed me out of the band. You're just lucky you haven't lost the others yet. It's only a matter of time."

By the time he finished talking, Randy stood directly in front of Rob.

"Are you two getting along?" Jason asked, walking over to them.

There was a moment of tension as Rob and Randy stood toe-to-toe staring into each other's eyes. Rob hated that he'd needed to call Randy. He regretted making the call, but he also knew it had been a necessary evil.

"We have a show starting in fifteen minutes," Jason continued. "How about you two put your macho bullshit aside for the next two hours while we rock the fucking house with Christmas music?"

The two didn't budge.

"It's Christmas Eve in Hallmark," Jason implored. "This is what this town was made for. Conflicts being set aside at the last minute. Rivalries put to rest. If you two can do that, it's better than the Christmas movies. It's not a sappy love story romance where you give each other the perfect gift as the snow falls. Fuck that. You two make up, let bygones be bygones, and we go out there and play music.

"Randy, plug in your guitar, work your fingers, and rip their faces off with your guitar shredding. Rob, grab that microphone, sing those lyrics, and make sure the crowd is headbanging until their necks break. Together, we can do this. We can make Hallmark Christmas Eve history. It's the first ever Merry Rock-Mas. Let's make them wish they'd been doing it for twenty years."

Both Rob Barrett and Randy St. James started nodding their head.

"Christmas music?" Randy asked.

"Christmas music," Rob answered.

"Is there a set list?"

"Eddie already had it taped to the stage. You can place your pedal board right next to it."

"Who's talking to us on the in-ears?"

"Mainly me," Jason said. "Stephanie is running the sound board and will be talking also."

"Just give me the key before each song," Randy said. Although his tone was relaxed, he still stood tall in front of Rob with his chest out. "I'll figure out the rest."

Rob shifted his gaze to Jason. "Get the others, will you?"

Jason scurried away without saying a word.

"I heard what you said," Rob said to Randy. "And you're right."

A moment later, Jason returned with Chad, Eddie, and Scott.

Rob took a deep breath. "Guys, I've got something I need to say before we go out on stage. I let my role in Sex Leppard get to my head. Without the rest of you, I'm just some guy screaming into a microphone. It takes all of us together to be a band.

"Tonight, it's not about me. It's not about what happens tomorrow or on New Year's Eve." With each phrase, his voice grew more intense. "It's about Christmas. It's about Hallmark. And it's about going out there and rocking the fucking house down."

"Yeah!" the five of them said in unity.

"Randy's agreed to fill in for Eddie tonight. I'd love to have him back full time, but that's up to him. By the way, it wouldn't mean that Eddie's out of the band. Just think about how bad ass we'd be with two electric guitars shredding it up. I'm getting a woody just thinking about it, but that's up to Randy if he'd like to be in, and up to the rest of you if you're okay with him being back."

Randy took a deep breath. "Ah fuck it. If you guys are okay with me coming back, I'd love to be a member of Sex Leppard again."

"What'll you do with Twisted Roses?" Jason asked.

"Fuck those guys. Posers."

Everyone laughed.

"I don't know about the rest of you," Chad said, brushing his long black hair behind his head. "But, once a Sex Leppard, always a Sex Leppard."

Smiles broke across each of their faces, and they all came in for a group hug.

Snow began falling all around them, dropping light flakes of white on their heads.

"What is it with this town and Christmas Eve?" Rob asked, shaking his head.

"It's a special place," Randy agreed.

Everyone stepped back, forming a circle. The other five gazed at Rob.

"What's everyone looking at me for?" he asked. "Randy, go get your shit set up and tuned. Eddie, take care of your hand. Jason, get your ass in the kit. Scott, loosen those fingers to tickle the ivories. Chad, well, you play bass so just stand in one place and nod."

Within a few minutes, everyone was in position. On the other side of the curtain, a packed amphitheater waited to have their heads blown away.

Rock 'N' Roll.

Christmas Rock 'N' Roll.

Merry fucking Rock-Mas!

A voice boomed from the PA system.

"Ladies and gentlemen, welcome to the first annual Merry Rock-Mas. Are you ready to rock?"

"Yes!" the crowd yelled.

The announcer asked louder, "Are you ready to rock?!"

"Yes!" the crowd screamed.

"It's time...for...Snow Leppard!"

The crowd erupted into yelling and applause.

The curtain pulled away. The lights shined down. Snow fell over the crowd.

Jason clicked his drumsticks together and yelled, "One, two, three, four."

Randy St. James hit the opening power chord with Chad laying a bass riff underneath. Scott blazed into an opening riff for "Oh Come All Ye Faithful" on the keyboard as Jason hammered on the drums.

Immediately, the crowd bounced their heads up and down in time to the music. They screamed and cheered.

When the opening riff ended, the band went silent. Rob grabbed the microphone and sang the first few lines acapella. Midway through the first verse, the band started building, driving the beat. They steadily intensified as Rob belted out the rest of the song, pausing for instrumental sections in between the verses.

They played classic Christmas song after classic Christmas song, each one adding in more metal and becoming heavier and heavier. Sex Leppard was back. The sonic wall of sound they created was unstoppable. Rob worked the stage, running over to Randy as he shredded on the guitar. His fingers flying over the fretboard like lightning. Rob ran over to Jason's drum kit, hitting the symbols with his bare hands in rhythm with the song.

The crowd ate it up. People no longer sat down in their seats, choosing to stand and headbang instead. Young and old, it didn't matter. The music entranced everyone. Captivated by the sound.

Just over halfway through the show, as Sex Leppard was at their peak, Rob knew it was time for the one they'd practiced the most. The one that pushed more sound, more volume, more pure sonic energy than any other song they had. He sat the microphone on its stand, quickly ran off stage, and came back with his own guitar strapped over his shoulder. A Flying V.

Jason clicked them off, and the band dove into "Carol of the Bells". Rob and Randy simultaneously strummed the opening power chord as Scott played the melody.

With the two electric guitars, the bass, and the drums hammering away, the heads of the crowd standing closest to the stage exploded. Their skulls ruptured, sending bone fragments and brain matter across the audience members behind them.

The band continued the chordal refrain, building the music to a grand intensity.

As the melody blazed on, another row of heads was blown away, splattering pieces of gray matter, eyeballs, and tongues into the crowd. Those that didn't explode had their skin torn off, leaving nothing but bloodied muscles and tendons.

As the song approached its ending, Rob's guitar stayed on the low power chords, while Randy's fingers flew to the higher notes, sending high pitched screams into the atmosphere, both from his guitar and from the audience.

Pacemakers exploded like grenades in people's chests, opening their ribcages like chest bursters from the *Alien* franchise. Hearing aids went off like dynamite inside of ear canals. The sides of heads were completely torn apart. Eyes fell out of open sockets. Fillings popped and shot teeth through people's cheeks with such force they impaled the heads of those in front of them; those whose heads hadn't already exploded.

Jason pounded away on the drums, driving the song to a massive climactic conclusion. With the final notes played, he hit one last crash on the symbol.

Silence filled the arena. The band glanced up from their instruments. Blood and carnage covered the Hallmark Amphitheater.

Rob turned to the rest of the band and smiled. "Hell, yeah! We fucking ripped their faces off!"

He heard something walk across the stage and turned around. At the base of the stage was Goliath with a ginger-bread man on each of his shoulders. The gingerbread men were clapping and cheering. Goliath held his hand up, his little fingers making the classic shape of devil horns.

"Rock on," Goliath said.

A Christmas Carol

S itting behind his large mahogany desk, Carlson Richards scanned a legal brief he'd received a few days earlier. Despite it being Christmas Eve, he toiled away in his office on Main. He hated coming to downtown Hallmark this time of year. All the lights, the garland, the festivities. It was all such a waste of taxpayer dollars.

In past years, as soon as Thanksgiving was over, he avoided downtown Hallmark like the plague that it was. He would've had his secretary, Julie Stephens, bring the file to him, but supposedly having your son stay for the holidays is reason to need Christmas Eve off. Carlson made a mental note to fire her tomorrow. That should be a nice present on Christmas morning.

His nose crinkled at the thought. That seemed to be as close as his face could get to a smile. As his eyes darted back and forth, he ran his fingers through what little gray hair he had left. He still wore his black suit jacket and a black overcoat, even within the confines of his office.

"May I adjust the thermostat?" Julie had asked him just yesterday. "At times, I think it's warmer outside than in here."

"If you think it's warmer outside, you are more than welcome to work from the sidewalk," he had snapped back. "The gas and electric bill are already too much. I will not indulge in the energy company's price gouging any more than I already do. If you're cold, might I suggest you wear something warmer than a cheap, ridiculous Christmas sweater? Those things are atrocious."

He had waved his hand to shoo her away, sending her back to finish her paperwork and filing, leaving him be.

Just outside of his office, the joyous sounds of Christmas songs forced their way in. "Deck the halls with boughs of holly," a deep male voice sang. A chorus of children chimed in with the "Fa la la"'s. More voices sang along as the noise outside grew louder and louder.

Frustrated, he tossed the papers down on his desk and shoved his chair back. He grabbed the cane that leaned against the wall behind him and stood up. A permanent scowl fixed across his face like lines carved into marble. Every time the cane struck the wooden floor, it sent an echoing thud throughout the office.

Carlson made his way from the office to the waiting area where Julie typically would be. The entry area had three beige chairs against the wall. A window displayed Main and the courthouse across the way.

Almost a hundred people gathered around the large Christmas tree.

"A shame," he said in his gruff tone. "Blocking the view of such a functional building as the courthouse with that fire hazard. A shame."

Another dozen people strolled past his window on their way to the candlelight ceremony.

"I'm never going to finish my work with all this ruckus outside," he told his reflection in the window. "Tomorrow will be quieter. Bah."

With the cane supporting his weight, he clomped back to his desk and shoved the papers back into their folder. He opened the top drawer of his desk, sat the folder inside, then locked it shut. With the file secured, he went to the coat rack in the corner. He removed his black fedora and gray scarf, tossed the scarf around his neck, and pushed the fedora down onto his head.

As he limped back into the waiting area, he saw more people, kids, families, all dressed in their Christmas wonderments, heading to the monstrosity of a tree across the street. Carlson took a deep breath and opened the door.

A faint sound of rock music drifted in the air. Carlson turned his nose up to it, debating on whether to file a noise complaint. Instead, head down, he stepped onto the sidewalk, pulled the door closed, and locked it. After stashing his keys back in his pocket, he hugged the side of the building, hoping to avoid contact with the throng soon to be enjoying their holiday revelry. All of them herded toward him as he tried to escape; he was a fish swimming upstream.

"Mr. Richards," a man said.

Carlson kept his head down and ignored him.

Undeterred, the man continued. "You should stick around for the candlelight ceremony."

Carlson's only answer was a mean-spirited grunt as he pushed past the man.

"You might just enjoy the festivities. Christmas cheer is contagious."

"Then get a vaccine for it," Carlson snapped back, barely turning around to respond. "Bah!" he scoffed.

Finally at his car, he crawled into the front seat, fired up the engine, and started to pull out of the parking lot. The stream of people made it impossible for him to jet onto the road. He waited for a small gap, and then shot his car onto Main, finally headed toward the peaceful solitude of his home.

After lighting the fireplace, Carlson Richards sat in his chair. He'd changed out of his black suit and into a pair of sweatpants, a sweater, and house slippers. His chair angled so the fire cast a reddish-orange glow across the pages of his book.

He stayed close to the fire. Just like in his office, he didn't want to turn up the heat. His house was huge. The largest on the block. One of the largest in Hallmark, if not the largest. Heating a home this size would cost a fortune. The energy companies just waited for saps who needed to turn the heat on. Instead, he opted for the age-old remedy. A nice, roaring fire in his large, stone fireplace. Cheaper, especially when he bought dried up Christmas trees for pennies.

As the fire crackled, he flipped from one page to the next. With his feet propped up on an ottoman, he rested his book on his knees while he read.

Next to him, he had a simple glass of gin. With each few turns of the page, he took a small sip. He hoped the combination of a warm fire, crackling wood, libations, and a nice read would help him drift off to slumber. Who needs Christmas Eve or even Christmas day? If it wasn't for his family connections, history, and business, he'd have left the overly festive town years ago. Don't think it didn't cross his mind. The closest he had come was after the fire.

His eyes drifted to the ceiling. Where the ceiling met the wall, light smoke stains could still be seen all these years later.

The fire had burned down a portion of the house. Unfortunately, it was the portion his wife and their baby boy had been in. It happened during the holiday season. A week before Christmas. Close enough that all the presents had been bought and the tree decorated. Mary took care of all the decorative stuff. She had enjoyed it. And since Carlson had worked late hours getting his practice up and running, it had given her something to do while he was gone.

That night, though, one of the strands of Christmas lights had sparked, according to the fire marshal. The tree had caught fire and spread down the hallway. The ME said both had died of smoke inhalation long before the fire reached them. Some bit of comfort through all the pain. At least they didn't feel their bodies burning to a crisp. At least they didn't realize as the roaring flames charred the skin from their bones.

Carlson Richards had to identify the bodies. It hadn't been challenging. Mary and Sebastian had been the only two people in the house. Her body had been found on the gliding rocker in the nursery, cradling their six-month-old son. He could picture what she had looked like. He'd come home so many times to wake her up in that same position so she could join him in bed.

Christmas lights and electrical cords wrapped around a dead tree. Why did anyone think that was a good idea?

He gave up sipping on his gin and tossed back the rest of the glass. He stared into the empty chalice, wishing it would magically refill itself.

"What do you say, Christmas magic?" he said. His voice echoed into the empty house. "Want to refill my glass? No? Bah! Nothing special about this town. Nothing special about this time of year. All commercialism and Hollywood fabrication."

After seriously contemplating throwing the glass into the fire, he sat it down gently on its tray. No point in being wasteful.

He sat the book down on the tray next to the glass and slipped down into the chair. He closed his eyes, ready to fall into a deep slumber until he heard a knock on his door.

"It's Christmas Eve," he yelled. "Let an old man sleep through the holidays in peace."

The rapping came again, and, after a brief pause, yet again.

"Bah! This had better be important," he said, grunting as he pushed himself out of the chair.

Another round of knocking on the door, this time louder and more furious.

"I'm coming," Carlson shouted as he hobbled to the door, favoring his back as he did.

He stepped into his foyer and opened the large wooden door.

"What do you want?" he snapped, but no one was there.

He gazed from one side of his dark lawn to the other but saw no one around. His foot hit something, and he peered down. A small brown box wrapped in sparkling Christmas wrapping paper sat on his front porch. Gingerly, he bent down and grabbed the box. A tiny note was affixed to the top of it, folded in half. With the box in his hands, he lifted the edge of the note and read. "Give and repent or join them in Hell."

"What sort of joyous Christmas message is this?" he shouted into the night. "Stupid kids and their holiday pranks."

He carried the gift back with him to his study. He eyed the small thing and started to open it, but then stopped himself. "Bah," he said and tossed the gift into the fireplace.

The fire briefly flared up before consuming the package.

Carlson Richards sat back in his chair, enjoying the warm glow and crackling sounds of the fireplace.

A loud series of thumps slammed against Carlson's front door, rousing him from a deep slumber. Startled, he nearly knocked over the tray with his book and the empty glass.

The fire had died down to nothing more than glowing embers.

At first, he thought he dreamt the whole thing. His heart raced in his chest. He placed his hand there and felt it pounding under his shirt. He tilted his head from side to side, stretching out his stiff neck.

Before he refound comfort, the loud knocking sounded again.

"I swear these kids playing pranks are going to be the death of me."

He stood up, grabbed his cane, and made his way slowly back to the door. Instead of ripping it open in a fury, he waited. Once the little brat knocked again, he'd catch them in the act. They wouldn't be able to run away this time.

As soon as the loud rapping hit the wooden door, he turned the knob and threw open the door.

A small, skinny boy stood on his front porch. The boy couldn't have been more than five or six. He wore blue jeans and a white T-shirt. His eyes were a deep blue, like staring into the ocean depths.

Richards wanted to yell at the boy, but his demeanor caught Carlson off guard. It was the way his innocent eyes stared at him. Carlson wasn't a sentimental person, most would say he was heartless, but those eyes held an unending sadness to them, like gazing at a decimated village inside of a snow globe, innocence and pain intertwined.

The boy held up a small package wrapped in the same sparkling Christmas wrapping paper as before. He didn't speak. He just held out the gift.

Carlson grabbed it. With the boy standing there, he couldn't just walk away and throw it into the fire again. He leaned his cane against the door frame and delicately separated the paper from the tape holding the wrapping together. He did it with great precision, taking care not to tear the paper. Once the paper was gone, he held a small cardboard box. He slipped his finger into the opening and carefully lifted the top.

A single blue pacifier, melted along the edges, sat in the box.

Carlson recognized it immediately. He remembered going to the Hallmark general store and purchasing the pacifier.

"Carl, he's teething," Mary had said. "When you go down the baby aisle, you'll see pacifiers specific for teething. Get a few of them. That way, if he gnaws through one, we'll have another."

"You think he'll gnaw through a pacifier?" he'd asked.

"I nurse him. Believe me. He has the capability."

He'd hurried off to the store. Just like Mary had told him, there were pacifiers specifically made for teething. Unfortunately, there was only one in stock. It had a blue ring on the top, connected to a blue mouth guard.

It was the same pacifier. Except the edges of the mouth guard were melted, as if they'd been through a...

"What kind of sick joke is this?" Carlson asked, peeling his eyes away from the box.

The boy had disappeared. He must've sprinted away while Carlson had drifted off into his memories.

He had no idea how the boy had known. As Carlson thought about it, the boy probably didn't. He had to be an errand boy for someone else. Who would've known about the pacifier? What kind of prankster was this? What happened those many years ago wasn't a secret. It'd been in the newspapers. It could be just a coincidence. They could've merely grabbed the same type of pacifier.

Carlson Richards curled his nose up in anger.

"Bah!" he yelled, releasing the built up tension.

He glanced once more across his front yard. The neighbor's Christmas lights provided the only glow, but those were far enough away to be barely noticeable. His yard was silent darkness.

Stepping back from the doorway with the box still in his hand, he slammed the door closed. The sound echoed throughout the empty house. Leaning on his cane, the old man hobbled back to the study. The fire had almost completely died out. He stared at the small pacifier once more, the melted edges around the mouthguard, and then tossed it into the smoldering red embers.

A whiff of smoke started around the cardboard. Within seconds, the porous kindling caught fire. The pacifier melted to nothing more than a glob of rubber and then disappeared under the ashes. Moments later, the entire gift was nothing more than ash.

Instead of falling asleep on the chair again, Carlson strode down the hallway, heading for his bedroom. As he reached the door, he heard another knock.

"Fuck off!" he shouted.

The knocking continued.

"If you don't leave me alone. I will call the police! Go bother someone else."

He burst into his bedroom and slammed the door behind him. The knocking didn't stop, but it was faint enough he could ignore it.

"You'll get tired and go away," he mumbled mostly to himself.

He pulled the covers back and crawled into bed, laying his head down on the soft feather pillow. As he closed his eyes, he recalled the boy at his door. Whoever was using him sure knew how to pick a sad face to deliver presents.

Carlson took a few deep breaths, relaxing himself, hoping the light drumbeat of knocking would lull him to sleep. His heart rate slowed, and he drifted off to sleep.

A dream crept into his head.

It was Christmas morning. Mary had Sebastian on her lap. Carlson sat next to the tree, passing out presents. He slid one over to Sebastian, and his little baby boy smiled a toothless smile. Mary clapped Sebastian's hands together, and his smile grew wider. Nothing but joy existed in his chubby little cheeks and perfect blue eyes.

Carlson reached behind the tree and pulled out a small package wrapped in sparkling Christmas wrapping paper. It was the same size as the package that had been left on his door twice that evening. It had a note on top. He glanced at the note. "Give and repent or join them in Hell."

As he read the note, he heard screaming. He glanced up and saw Mary and Sebastian, covered in flames. They screamed in pain as their skin roasted, melting together as it did, fusing the two into one. His heart pounded in his chest. Pounded so hard he could hear it. The pounding grew louder and louder until...

Carlson sat up right, drenched in sweat. The pounding became a knocking on his door. Someone was banging on his bedroom door. They were inside his house.

He slid out of bed, reached into his nightstand, and grabbed his gun. With his cane in one hand and his gun in the other, he stumbled to the door. After a few deep breaths, he let go of the cane and jerked open the bedroom door.

No one was there. The hallway was empty. No one was there but him.

A knock hammered against his front door.

Frustrated and furious, he grabbed his cane and made his way to the front door. With the gun still in his hand, he did the same thing. He laid the cane against the wall and threw open the door.

The same boy stood there. He was still dressed in blue jeans and a white T-shirt, but his clothes appeared to be covered in ashes and soot. His cheeks had burn patches on them, and his arms were scarred. But those eyes, they were the same, with the same deep sorrow.

"Leave!" he shouted into the boy's face.

The boy held up a small box wrapped in Christmas wrapping paper. The same wrapping paper that had haunted him all night.

"You want me to take the present? I already know what it is," he sneered.

Carlson yelled into the dark over the boy's head. "Whoever is doing this, you're sick! Go back to whatever hellhole you crawled out of and leave me alone!"

He snatched the gift from the boy's hands and tore off the wrapping paper. As he did, he stared at the boy, making sure the child didn't run off again. He tore the top of the box off with the wrapping paper shredded at his feet. He reached in to grab the pacifier. However, what he found was much smaller.

Surprise took his eyes away from the boy. His fingers hadn't landed upon a hard, rubbery pacifier, but the sharp edge of a diamond, set on top of a ring. He gripped the diamond between his fingertips and lifted it out of the box.

Immediately, he flipped it over, searching for the initials and date. They were there. His hand shook. The last time he'd seen this ring was when he handed it to the funeral director to be buried with his wife.

Carlson dropped the gun he'd been holding as he fell against the door frame. The world wobbled. The pacifier could've been a lucky guess, but this? They would've had to exhume Mary's body to have gotten this ring.

He shook his head in disbelief.

He backed into the entryway and closed the door, not caring if the boy still stood on the front porch or not. His eyes never left the ring. He blindly searched for his cane, and when he finally found it, gripped the top of it. Part of him hoped holding it in his hand might anchor him back in reality. A reality where he wasn't holding the engagement ring he had given Mary those decades ago. The ring he buried with her. The ring with his and Mary's initials and the date he proposed to her.

One step at a time, he found his way back to the study. If not for sheer muscle memory, he wouldn't have made it back to his chair next to the now-dormant fireplace.

He collapsed into the chair, his eyes never leaving the ring.

Carlson felt reality slipping away. Was this senility? Reality and dream mixing into one? Reality and nightmare?

He missed Mary and Sebastian. What would he have become if they were still alive? If that damned Christmas light never set the tree ablaze? If they hadn't died in that

God-forsaken fire? Would he still be the grumpy old man half the town hoped would die soon anyway?

Light footsteps ventured from the entry way into his study. Carlson didn't need to turn around to know who it was. He knew. Once he made the connection, the eyes had given him away. Those deep blue eyes that had once upon a time been filled with such joy. Eyes that had filled his own heart with such happiness.

"Why are you here?" he asked. The fury had left his voice. Instead, he fought to speak through his grief, from choking back tears.

"Look at me," Sebastian said.

Carlson shook his head. "I don't want to look. I want to remember you how you were."

"Look at me," Sebastian demanded.

Slowly, the old man turned his head.

Sebastian's face was a scorched mess. Burnt pieces of flesh flaked away. No skin had been left untouched by the fire. His hair was gone. Red embers still blazed down his arms and across his forehead like veins. His blue eyes were the only thing that resembled the boy who had first knocked on his door that night. It was his son, grown up at least ten years beyond when he died, despite having died decades before.

"You're the reason I'm burning in Hell. She and I both are burning in Hell because of you."

"No, no you're not," Carlson argued, shaking his head.

"You're constant despising of everything we loved, everything you were, the hatred that burns in your heart, the blame that you cannot extinguish has left us like this."

"I'll repent. I'll change."

Sebastian reached his smoldering hand toward Carlson. "We'll see what burns in your heart." He touched his father's forehead.

Carlson found himself on his back inside of a wooden box. The top of the box hovered inches above his nose, and the sides of the box pressed up against his arms. He tried to raise his head, but his forehead hit the lid. He was trapped, pinned down, and unable to move.

The darkness within was all consuming.

Panic began to take hold. He knew what a coffin looked like. He'd buried enough people and seen enough movies to know. But this wasn't a nice, elegant coffin like the one he had already pre-purchased for himself. There was no cushioned lining to sleep away eternity in style. This was simply a wooden box like what he'd seen in the old west movies. A pine box that barely fit him.

Breathing became harder. His chest tightened. He'd never considered himself claustrophobic before, but he had also never laid in his own coffin before.

Through tiny slivers in the wood by his feet, small streams of light slipped inside. The light gave off a soft glow. As soon as the light started, the coffin began to move. A rumbling sensation reverberated across his back as if he was being carried along a conveyor belt. The coffin moved toward the glowing light, and as the light became more intense, heat radiated.

Crematorium, he thought. *I'm being burned alive.*

"Wait!" he shouted. "I'm alive in here. Wait!"

The inside of the coffin went from cozily warm to unbearably hot. Sweat broke out across his body. The soles of his shoes melted down the bottom of his feet. The rubber scalded his heels. Fire erupted inside of the coffin.

Carlson tried to kick, but there was no room for his legs to bend. His sweatpants caught fire. He smelled burning wool along with burning flesh. Searing pain traveled up his legs, and he screamed. He tried to bang on the coffin, but in the tight confinement, he couldn't gain enough leverage to make a noticeable sound.

The fire spread up his legs and waist. The pain was unbearable. He wished he would pass out from it or from a lack of oxygen. Something to take the pain away.

His eyes tried to produce tears, but they evaporated in the heat the moment they left his eyes. Fire spread to his chest. His arm and chest hair curled and singed. His legs didn't hurt anymore. Once the nerve endings burned away, the pain stopped. But he knew they still burned, the skin cooking away into blackened chunks.

"I'm sorry!" he yelled. "I'm sorry I couldn't save you. I'm sorry my life has been filled with hate and resentment." More tears tried to escape, immediately boiling from his face. "I'm going to change," he cried. "I'm going to change. I'm going to..."

He kicked and awoke in his bed, violently flailing his arms from side to side. His covers lay strewn to one side. He set up straight and grabbed the clock on his nightstand.

"Ten thirty!" he shouted. "It's ten thirty! It's still Christmas Eve."

He threw his legs over the side of the bed, grabbed his cane, and stood up. Joy spread through him. Joy that he hadn't felt in years. He had been given another chance. A chance to repent. A chance to be a better person than the one he had been all these years.

For the first time in ages, he smiled. With his cane supporting him, he strode from his bedroom and down the hallway. He didn't stop to grab a coat, wanting to hurry outside.

He flung open the door. It was snowing. Snowing on Christmas Eve. He loved Hallmark. He couldn't imagine a better place than this little festive town, especially during the holidays. A place of Christmas magic and second chances.

Within a few steps, he was down his front porch and on his sidewalk. The snow fell against his face and on his clothes. Except, the snow wasn't cold, and it wasn't melting.

Carlson held his hand out, catching some of it. He tasted a sampling while looking at the flakes in his hand.

It wasn't snow; it was ash. Ash fell from the sky. Somewhere in the distance, a huge fire burned.

Carlson froze, confused, but then heat resonated from his feet. He glanced down in time to see his feet spontaneously burst into flames. The fire quickly traveled up his feet to his pants legs and all the way to his waist before he had time to register what was happening.

His panicked eyes lifted and saw Sebastian and Mary standing at the door to the house. Sebastian pointed and laughed at him. Mary joined in.

"There's no salvation for you," he said. "No repentance. No forgiveness. Time to burn with us in Hell."

Carlson Richards ran as fast as his old legs would take him back toward the house. Back to Mary and Sebastian. The skin of his legs burned away, fusing the wool sweatpants with his raw muscle tissue. The flames traveled up his shirt, wrapping his entire body into one big candle flame.

He ran back up the steps and fell into the house, catching the floor on fire as the hellish flames consumed his body.

O Christmas Tree

"Kids, stop chasing the gingerbread men!" Todd yelled at Grace and Chris.

Chris was ten, and Grace was seven. Despite their father's objection, they ran through the park, weaving around the growing crowd, chasing after the little demon cookies.

The Hallmark Christmas Tree towered over them. They hadn't been this close to the tree before. The tree rose over seventy feet in the air. Christmas lights encircled it, and large ornaments dangled from the branches.

"Chris! Grace! Stay with us," Hannah shouted. "There are way too many people for you to be wandering off."

In the distance, Chris heard music playing. It sounded like "Joy to the World", but with a lot of electric guitar. He'd seen a flyer about the concert and had wanted to go, but his dad said they were going to the candlelight ceremony instead. Something about loud music not being good for their ears, blah blah blah. To him, it sounded awesome.

Hordes of townsfolk from all around Hallmark streamed around the courthouse and in front of the Christmas tree. By the looks of it, there had to be over five hundred people already there.

Chris eyed his little sister. "Tag," he said, and took off running.

"Not fair," Grace shouted, then ran after him.

"Gracey," Hannah yelled in patented mom voice. "You and your brother need to stay with us."

"But, mommy," Grace whined. "Chris tagged me. I have to tag him or I'm it. I don't want to be it."

"I don't care," Hannah said. "Soon, they're going to pass out candles and turn the lights off. You don't want to be separated from us when it gets dark."

"It's not fair," Grace pouted. "Everyone else gets to run around and have fun. Why can't we?"

Chris ran up beside Todd. Both parents stood between the two siblings. Chris stuck his tongue out at Grace and shook his head, taunting her.

"Dad," Chris said. "Some of my friends are playing over there. Can I please go? I'll be back before they turn the Christmas tree lights off."

Todd glanced over at Hannah.

Reluctantly, Todd answered, "That's fine. But you have to take your sister as well. No fighting. And don't forget, it's Christmas Eve. Santa's watching. You don't want to end up on the naughty list."

"Don't worry," Chris said. "We'll behave."

Chris took Grace's hand and sprinted to the far side of Hallmark's town square.

"Don't end up on the naughty list," Chris mocked. He turned to his little sister. "Santa's not even real."

"Yes, he is," Grace argued. "He brought me that bike last year."

"No, you baby. Santa isn't real. Mom and Dad bought the bike for you and slapped Santa's name on it. Grow up."

Grace kicked Chris in the shin. "I'm not a baby. You're the baby."

"Ow, you little turd," Chris said, reaching for his shin. "You're going to go on the naughty list for that."

"Well, you're going to go on the naughty list for saying Santa isn't real."

"He's not. Santa and his naughty list can kiss...my...ass."

Grace's chin dropped, and her mouth hung open in shock. "I'm telling. You cursed."

"It's in the Bible, so it should be fine to say. Ass. Damn. Hell." Chris stuck his tongue out at his sister.

She kicked him again, turned, and ran away.

Chris ran after her.

He dodged around people waiting for the ceremony to begin. The crowd grew thicker as more people arrived. A few times, Chris crunched a gingerbread man as he tried to catch his sister.

Grace turned a corner, and he did the same. Suddenly, both stopped and stared up at a big red suit. Santa Claus stared down at them with an unhappy look on his face.

"Are you two behaving?" he asked.

"Cram it," Chris said and punched his sister in the arm. "That's for kicking my leg."

"It's not nice to hit," Santa said. "Hitting can get you on the naughty list."

"Stop the act. I know Santa's not real, even if my baby of a sister still believes." Chris crossed his arms, acting bigger than he was.

"I'm not a baby," she yelled at Chris. "I don't believe in Santa either. Delivering all the presents in one night is impossible."

"But that's Christmas magic," Santa said.

"Our parents already got us our gifts, so why should we worry about some naughty list?"

"You two should go back to your parents. You could get lost once the tree lights go out. They'll be going out in just a few more minutes."

Grace glanced at her brother. She touched him and said, "Tag," and then sprinted away, immediately swallowed by all the people waiting for candles.

"Cheater!" Chris yelled and ran after her.

With the crowd swarming, Chris slowed down and then came to a stop. He peered one direction, then another, expecting to see Grace somewhere, but he couldn't find her. He slowly paced back the way he came. All he could see were people's backs. He craned his neck higher and saw the top of the Christmas tree. They had wound up on the opposite side of the courthouse.

"Grace!" he hollered. "Where are you?"

"You lost your sister," a condemning voice said.

Chris spun but couldn't tell where the voice came from.

"That's sure to get you on the naughty list. Think you can find her? I bet you can't. Not before the lights go out."

Chris saw the remaining candles passed out. Person after person had a candle in their hand. He knew once everyone had a candle, the Christmas lights would turn off, plunging the town square into darkness. Then, slowly, the candles would be lit. He needed to find Grace and fast.

"It's the naughty list for you. Just like it was the naughty list for your sister. Kids who don't listen to their parents, kids who kick and punch, those are bad kids. Bad kids are on the naughty list."

"Who's saying that?" Chris asked. Tears welled up in his eyes. "Where's my sister? Where is she?"

He shuffled through the crowd and rubbed tears from his eyes. He glanced behind him, searching for Grace when he bumped into someone. He quickly spun and stared up into the face of Santa Claus.

Just as he did, Hallmark's town square went dark.

Todd held his candle and Chris's. Hannah held hers and Grace's.

"Any idea where they are?" Todd asked.

"No. Hopefully, they didn't end up on the naughty list this close to Christmas. They were decent all year long. Now they're going to lose it on Christmas Eve? That'd really stink. How much longer until the lights go out?"

Todd glanced at his watch. "About two more minutes. Hey, the concert must be over. I'm not hearing music."

"Assuming Hallmark timed everything right, it should end just before this starts. I'd hate to compete against a band as we sing carols," Hannah said.

"You're assuming Hallmark timed everything right on Christmas Eve? Honey, of course they did. It's Hallmark. At Christmas time. Everything will work out perfectly just like it always does."

"Speaking of perfect, did you see that Harper Reed and Brandon Harris got back together? She'd moved to New York City but decided to stay here after her dad passed."

"I heard," Todd said. "Brandon told us about it at the station. By the way, have you seen Yvonne around? The gingerbread men have played havoc on vehicles, and she isn't responding to calls."

Hannah shrugged her shoulders. "She had dinner with an attractive young man the other night. Maybe they hit it off, and he whisked her away to some castle."

Todd chuckled. "Oh please, like that sounds like her."

"Do you want to go look for the kids?" Hannah asked.

"What's the point? The lights are about to go out. It's too late."

Just as Todd answered, all of Hallmark went dark. The entire crowd went silent. Snowflakes began to fall, setting the perfect Christmas mood.

Todd and Hannah dropped the candles they held for Chris and Grace. Todd reached for Hannah's hand instead.

A small candle was lit from the base of the Christmas tree. That candle lit another. The two became four, and the four became eight. Exponentially, the number of lit candles spread. A light glow illuminated the crowd. Faces basked in shades of orange, red, and yellow.

As the candlelight grew, the choir standing on a stage away from the giant Christmas tree began to sing.

"Oh Christmas Tree, Oh Christmas Tree."

Slowly, members of the crowd joined in.

"How lovely are your branches."

"Oh Christmas Tree, Oh Christmas Tree, how lovely are your branches."

"It's lovely, isn't it?" Hannah asked.

"Too bad the kids aren't here to watch," Todd said.

"Well, they're on the naughty list, so I'm sure their view is better than ours."

"You're right." Todd nodded his head in agreement.

"Not only green in summer's heat," they both belted out. "But also winter's snow and sleet. O Christmas tree, O Christmas tree, how lovely are your branches!"

The choir led them in the second and third verse. With each refrain of "O Christmas Tree", more joined in until everyone standing on the town square and on the surrounding streets sang loudly. Hundreds of voices sang in unison by candlelight.

As the snow fell across the courtyard, the song came to an end. The choir took a step backward, and Santa Claus stepped onto the stage with a candle in his hand. No one applauded or yelled in honor of the occasion's somberness. Everyone drew closer together. A town in solitude and harmony. Hallmark was at its most magical.

"On this night of Christmas Eve," Santa said. "We remember why we celebrate. We remember the joy of giving, of kindness, of goodness, and of decency. It's about the happiness you can spread to others. Whether it's those in true need, or those who just need a quick 'Hi' on a Monday morning. Joy can be found wherever you look. It just takes opening your hearts and your eyes to find it.

"Christmas isn't about being selfish. It's not about what you can get but what you can give others. It's not about doing what you want but doing what you need. Doing what you want, not listening when you should, misbehaving. Those will get you on my naughty list, and, of course, no one wants to be on the naughty list, especially on Christmas Eve.

"Now, as the snow falls during this magical night, I'll ask everyone to join the choir in singing this last song. I wish you all a Merry Christmas and an extremely Happy Holidays."

Santa moved to the side of the stage as the choir advanced to the front. One soloist stepped closer than the others. She took a deep breath.

"Silent night. Holy night," she sang. Her voice reverberated off the surrounding buildings. It sounded like a chorus of angels. The echo mimicked that of a large cathedral. "All is calm. All is bright."

As she sang the song, Santa, with his lit candle in hand, strode to the Christmas tree. Those at the front of the crowd did as well.

Stacks of wooden pallets and loose kindling made up the base of the seventy-foot pine tree. It held the tree in place but also appeared as a natural sloping landscape.

Santa tossed the candle onto the kindling base.

"Round yon Virgin Mother and Child."

Others slowly filed around the tree, careful to keep their candle lit and avoid touching anyone else with it. As each person approached the tree, they tossed their lit candle onto the base.

"Holy infant so tender and mild."

The candles' flames ignited the kindling. The organizers had doused the base with an accelerant. Instead of the kindling smoking or smoldering, a noticeable flame sprang up after the first few candles had been tossed. With each passing moment, the fire grew bigger and bigger.

"Sleep in heavenly peace. Sleep in heavenly peace."

Heat emanated from the base and rose up the tree, seeking branches for more fuel. The whole area brightened with the ever-expanding, ever-growing light source. The air filled with the smell of smoke and pine. Todd and Hannah stepped closer and closer as the crowds in front of them tossed their candles and moved away.

The soloist took a few steps back to join the rest of the choir. The entire chorus began the second verse as the sound of crackling fire continued behind them. Their voices filled the atmosphere with joyous song as the entire base became engulfed in flame.

It was Todd and Hannah's turn. They went as close as they could to the inferno. Todd felt hairs on his arms singe from the radiating heat. As he tossed the candle, he heard Chris's voice.

"Dad!" Chris shouted.

"Daddy, help!" Grace yelled.

Todd peered up and tapped Hannah's arm. All the large ornaments on the tree started thirty feet up and continued to the top. Todd pointed to an ornament suspended forty feet above them. It was shaped like a large sphere, but instead of a glass ball, it was made of wrought iron. In the middle, trapped in the large cage, sat Chris and Grace. Todd glanced from one ornament to the next. Some were empty, but most contained children.

Chris and Grace stared down at their parents.

"Mommy! Daddy! Help us! We're sorry," Chris pleaded. "We can be good. We promise we can."

Hannah waved at the children trapped in the cage, and then shook her head. "Poor things are on the naughty list."

"We told them to behave."

"And on Christmas Eve, no less."

Todd turned his head back to his children. "Bye, kids. Try not to scream too loud. We enjoy the singing."

"Silent Night. Holy Night," Todd and Hannah sang, adding their voices to the multitude around them.

FRIENDS AT A DINER

The roar of the motorcycle dies down to a purr before finally stopping completely. His leathers creak as he dismounts. The heel strikes of his boots echo on the sidewalk. His eyes glance at the other motorcycles parked next to him. As he reaches the diner's small glass door, he pushes it open. A bell rings, announcing his presence.

Three men sit at a table in the middle of the deserted diner. One of them has his feet propped up on an empty chair, leaning back. A carafe of coffee sits in the center of the table.

"What took you so long?" War asks.

"I wasn't through playing yet," Death says, pointing out the window of the diner.

All four of them turn and stare in that direction.

A man dressed as Santa frantically runs down the road. His face is covered in blood. Splotches of dark crimson cover the suit. He cries for help, stumbling as he tries to escape his pursuers.

"Mr. Fields," Prince Vlad says. He is two dozen feet away from Santa Claus. "Fetch my Christmas dinner."

"Of course, Your Majesty," Jonathan replies, standing next to his prince.

With a baseball bat in hand, Jonathan sprints to the festively dressed man, quickly gaining on him. Jonathan raises the bat over his head and swings just as he catches up with Santa. The bat connects with Santa's head, and the man collapses to the ground.

"Don't kill him, Mr. Fields. You know I prefer a fresh dinner, especially on special occasions."

Jonathan leans down and checks Santa's pulse.

"He's alive." Jonathan grabs Santa's leg and drags him. "When I get him in the trunk, I'll bind him better, Your Highness."

"Thank you, Jonathan."

The Prince turns and struts back to the car, leaving Jonathan to drag the heavy body. He tosses a glance at the diner and waves.

The four men watching wave back.

"Saint Nick was annoying," Death says.

He strides to the empty chair and gazes down at Pestilence's boots comfortably resting there. Death kicks Pestilence's legs, and with a sour look on his face, Pestilence drops his feet down to the ground.

"Thank you," Death says and sits down.

Outside, snow falls and begins to accumulate. It blankets the area in white. Everything except the four motorcycles. Those remain untouched, generating their own heat and melting the snow before it ever reaches them. The towering inferno that was once Hallmark's large Christmas tree adds an evening glow on the Christmas Eve horizon.

A gingerbread man hops onto the table and eyes the four. Before it can escape, Famine grabs it and eats it, devouring the whole cookie.

"Gingerbread is my favorite," he says. "Those little guys are tasty."

"Every time the four of us get together," War says, "the whole area goes to shit."

Death smiles. "My favorite is when we meet up during the holidays. This town and its reputation, though." He lifts his hand to his mouth and kisses his fingertips. "Chef's kiss."

Pestilence leans forward onto the table. "How about next year, Famine and I get a chance to have some fun?"

"Didn't you two get your jollies in 2019 and 2020?" War asks.

"That was fun," Pestilence says with a fond smile. "Hadn't had fun like that in almost a century. But it wasn't like you guys just sat around doing nothing. Death dabbled. And War, you're always stirring up trouble somewhere."

"Alright," Death says. "Next time the four of us hang out, you two can spread your own brand of torment."

Something outside the window catches Death's eye. The Hallmark Christmas tree wobbles on its weakened trunk and collapses to the ground. A filling sensation in his soul means that more have just died. A lot more. He takes a large gulp of coffee.

"Well, I'm heading out. Time to put Hallmark out of its misery. I've been here for a week and am ready to see this town from my rear-view mirrors. All the niceties are making me sick to my stomach. Who should I blame for that? You, Pestilence?"

The quartet laughs. "I don't do niceties," Pestilence says. "Prefer the boils and the blood vomit."

Death stands up from the table. "War. Famine. Pestilence. Text the group any pictures you took. I'll do the same and I do have some good ones. Other than that, text me the next time you guys want to ride together." He pauses for a moment. "Famine, I said text. Don't call. Nobody does that shit anymore."

"Fuck off, Death," Famine snaps but with a smile.

Death marches back to the door. He opens it, and the bell announces his departure. A few moments later, he's sittin on his pale motorcycle and revs the engine, drowning out the sweet sound of screams.

He backs out of the diner's gravel parking lot and hits the road. The presence of his brothers grow less and less.

The further away he drives, the more their effect on Hallmark dissipates. He eases the motorcycle into the middle of the road, aligning his tires directly onto the center stripe. He sits upright and extends his arms out to his side, gripping the vehicle with only his thighs. He closes his eyes and transports his consciousness to Hallmark.

Fire spreads throughout downtown Hallmark from the toppled Christmas tree. Bodies, their skin charred black, cover the streets. Realization washes over the survivors as the four riders go their separate ways. Panic and chaos rips through the remaining few.

"Chris! Grace!" Todd screams, searching for his lost children. He has a vague memory of them playing near the tree, but not what happened after.

He glances up and sees Brandon Harris, bloodied and screaming. Part of his cheek is carved away. Todd can see Brandon's teeth. Behind him, Harper Reed carries a knife in one hand and the head of a little girl in the other. Harper stares at Brandon with murderous intent behind her eyes.

Screams and wails of agony reverberate around Hallmark. The town erupts into crazed chaos. From the amphitheater where rivers of blood flow down the grassy hill to the home of a lonely librarian where a mutilated corpse with permanent dimples sewn into his face lies next to her in her bed.

Death smiles, wondering if this is the end of the cliche, cheesy Christmas movies this town inspires. He doubts it. People have a way of always finding joy in life. Finding hope. Especially at Christmas.

Death rides on a pale motorcycle into the darkness.

To Hell with Hallmark.

A Final Gift From Me To You

'Twas the Nightmare Before Christmas

'Twas the night before Christmas, when all through the house

Not a creature was stirring, not even a mouse.

Our living room was decorated and the fireplace aglow

The outside was frigid, and everywhere snow.

My parents lay cuddled, all snuggled in bed,

And I waited up to see Santa instead.

As the night grew colder, the fireplace it died

In the cold winter night, a stranger I spied.

I jumped from the couch and wiped frost from the glass,

Through the window I stared past the white winter grass.

The only light that shone 'cross the snow-covered land,

Came from the moon, the late-night hour at hand.

Can you guess what my weary eyes rested 'pon?

It wasn't St. Nick, but the devil's own spawn.

It stood in the lawn, and gazed at the house

Then leapt to the sky with a single quick bounce.

It flew in the air, on the roof it did land.

In fear I was frozen, all my hairs they did stand.

Above me I could hear it walking around

Trying to get inside this house that it found.

I ran to the couch and hid under the covers

Hoping it wouldn't be me it discovered.

Claws they clicked, down the chimney they came,

Frozen with fright, I couldn't shout or proclaim.

Suddenly it arrived, from the fireplace it entered

Basked by the lights, its features were rendered.

Its eyes were black, as black as the night

And its teeth were sharp, how they glistened in light.

Its skin was green and covered in scales,

and hands were claws with sharp razor nails.

The tongue slithered out o'er the fangs in his mouth

Red and grotesque, it flicked all about.

My young mind it hoped and continuously prayed

That this was the Grinch, so don't be afraid.

The black eyes stared at the lights on the tree,

A deep glow abiding in a vast and dark sea.

And there as I stared at the creature in fear,

It picked up its head as there was something to hear.

From the staircase I heard the stomping of feet,
The creature then turned as it smelled some fresh meat.
Before I could warn whoever was there,
It sprang up the stairs and started to tear.
A pool of thick blood on the floor it did spread,
Even the white walls quickly turned red.
My father lay bloodied at the top of the stairs,
His eyes looked down; his insides laid bare
The green beast continued, up the steps it went.
I started to cry. I cowered and wept.
It didn't take long before the screams they did start,
Moments later, it returned, chewing a heart.
Finally without warning, its eyes saw me crying,
Its mouth did widen, a smile no denying.
Between its sharp fangs filled with blood and with gore,
I knew in that moment, my life was no more.
Each step that it took, the claws clicked and they scraped
'cross the stairs and the floor, its mouth all agape.
It stood o'er the top of me, and in the seat as I set,
My bladder let go, and the couch I did wet.
From deep in the guttural throat of this Grinch,
I heard a wretch'd sound that caused me to flinch.

Laughter sprang forward from its scaly, green face,
It leaned back its head and cackled in place.

It must've thought this was funny that I pissed on myself,

But what else could I have done before this evil elf?

Right past me it went and to the chimney it stood,

Before grabbing a Santa hat and dawning the hood.

One last glance my direction, it shot me a look,

Then sprang up the chimney as if straight from a book.

I couldn't move you see, I was frozen in place.

Knowing I'd never forget the look on its face.

As I sit here penning the story that occurred,

Hoping for Peace, though that's probably absurd.

Can you guess what happened on that cold Christmas
morn?

I was locked away, and from my home I was torn.

The authorities believed I slaughtered my parents.

Guess they figured I did not like my presents.

And now on this night with me grown and now old,

I stare through iron bars and watch over the cold.

Each year I do wonder on December Twenty and Five,

Why did that evil Grinch leave me alive?

ACKNOWLEDGEMENTS

As usual, I must first thank my wonderful wife, Terri. She has been and continues to be my rock while writing. She continues the task of reading and editing my first draft. The first time around, these stories are not near as delightful.

Thank you to my grandmother, Jessie Kruger. It was while watching Hallmark Christmas movies with her during Christmas 2023 that the concept of this book was born. She passed away Jan 28, 2024, before I wrote this book, but I know she would have gotten a laugh out of reading these.

Thank you, Crystal Baynam and the team at Unveiling Nightmares, for publishing this anthology.

Thank you, Christy Aldridge, for the magnificent cover art. I love the gingerbread men!

Thank you, Krista Snyder, Courtney Deguire, and everyone else at Blackbird Books and Spirits. The excitement on your faces every time I spoke about this project helped provide the motivation to complete it as fast as I did.

And as always, thank you, constant reader, for hanging out for a bit inside of my head. You were great company. I hope you enjoyed reading this as much as I enjoyed writing it.

Until next time.

About the Author

Brad is the author of the upcoming novels "Fear Not The Dead" (Unveiling Nightmares, 2024) and "The Night Crew" (Crystal Lake Publishing, 2025). He has a short story published in "Body Horror Anthology, bk 1" (Unveiling Nightmares, 2024).

Brad lives in Central Texas with his wife Terri. Together, they have 5 kids that keep them constantly busy.

During the day, he is an Account Manager for an online software company. At night, he enjoys listening to the little voices in his head and jotting down the stories they tell him.

A lifelong fan of Horror, Brad pulls inspiration from everyone from Edgar Allan Poe to Stephen King.

.

Printed in the USA
CPSIA information can be obtained
at www.ICGtesting.com
LVHW022035241124
797512LV00001B/59